INDENTURED DAUGHTER

CAROLYN FAULKNER

Published by Blushing Books
An Imprint of
ABCD Graphics and Design, Inc.
A Virginia Corporation
977 Seminole Trail #233
Charlottesville, VA 22901

Indentured Daughter
Carolyn Faulkner

eBook ISBN: 978-1-63954-510-0
Print ISBN: 978-1-63954-511-7

Chapter 1

"NO." Flat. Definitive. Non-negotiable, just like the three others he'd already given her.

But it had to be. It just had to!

Lavinia Montclaire shifted nervously in what had looked like a comfortable seat when she'd first sat down, barely able to believe his response. But it wasn't the chair that had her heart beating so strongly and quickly within her chest that she was feeling a bit faint.

Is this what the vapors were like? she wondered. She'd never succumbed to them herself—and frankly looked askance at women who used them with alarming regularity, along with other women's complaints—to avoid unpleasant situations or people they didn't like.

She frowned, confounded by his annoyingly implacable demeanor.

What honorable man would decline a lady's sincere request?

And, more than that, why would any man want to marry a woman who didn't want to marry him, and had—essentially—just told him as much?

"Was there something else I could help you with, Vinnie?" he asked, leaning forward and making her feel suddenly crowded in what was his surprisingly small office. "I know I didn't give you much time before the wedding, so I imagine you and your mother have a lot to do in order to get ready before Friday."

Startled by what he'd revealed, she did her best to hide her surprise. Her parents had said that she was to marry him, but they hadn't mentioned a date—she certainly would have remembered it if they had! They probably intended to spring that on her, too!

But her face darkened further as his dark chocolate voice flowed slowly over her body, sparking lingering—if very reluctant—fires here and there, mostly there.

She forced herself to ignore those errant feelings and concentrate on her anger—at the fact that she was apparently to be forced into marrying him, a sacrificial lamb sold to the devil in order that her parents could continue to live in the style to which they were accustomed.

But that was old anger—comparatively—and she was surprised to realize that what she was the unhappiest about at the moment was that he was—she suspected—being deliberately over-familiar with her. Only family, and close family at that, ever used that particular nickname with her.

They'd never met before, that she could recall, which was one of her objections, in a long line of them. And she would be willing to bet dollars to doughnuts that he, too, would have been perfectly be happy to have them introduced when they met before the priest, once she'd walked down the aisle at their wedding!

But she wisely didn't think that taking him to task about what would probably be a trivial matter to him—as much as she wanted to—would help her achieve her goal, so she bit her usually sharp tongue nearly through rather than giving him what for about that, or indeed, anything else on her list.

Instead, Lavinia forced herself to relax as much as she could, considering the gravity of the situation, but he didn't make it easy. She took a deep breath, knowing she was going to have to play the ace she had up her sleeve. The fact that she'd only just gotten there a few minutes ago and she was already at the point of last resort didn't bode well for the success of this little endeavor, but she had no choice.

She had to get him to agree to break their "engagement"—such as it was. The one she hadn't been told about until a day or so ago, that had been arranged by her parents without so much as a by-your-leave from her.

Vinnie took a deep breath and forged on, her hopes fading the longer she sat there with him looking at her as if he'd like to make a meal of her.

"Well, I do have some money of my own that I inherited from my grandmother. I don't think my parents remember— or maybe even know—that I have it."

His dark eyebrow rose. "Oh? And how much might that be?"

"Two thousand dollars," she informed him, expecting his eyes to light up at the enormous sum.

But they didn't. Instead, Sterling Winters, Lord Glastonbury of Arbor Hall, leaned back in his chair, his intense gaze settling on her like a physical touch, from which she had to prevent herself from cringing.

"Two thousand, you say?"

Why did she feel like a mouse between a cat's paws at a moment when she should have felt triumphant, having solved both her own—and her family's—highly distasteful problem.

"Have your parents talked to you about their current situation at all, Vinnie?"

Surprised at the question, she answered honestly, "No. It's rude and gauche to discuss finances."

His lordship's broad smile was far from reassuring or even pleasant. In fact, it—and his tone—contained a note of censure that he didn't bother to try to curb. "Perhaps if your parents had had a rude, gauche, and frank discussion with you about money—or rather their distinct lack thereof—you might not find yourselves in such a bleak situation."

Disbelievingly, she asked, "Are you suggesting that *I* am the cause of my parents' financial distress?"

Without so much as a nod in her direction, he flipped open a large box on his desk and withdrew a slim cigar, lighting it before he sat back again.

The smell wasn't at all unpleasant, but then, the smell had never been her problem. It was the lack of manners he displayed in not asking her if she minded if he smoked that set her temper even further on edge, not to mention the fact that the smoke itself would play hell with her lungs.

Not that she was about to reveal that, or indeed, any other weakness to this man, even if she ended up fainting breathlessly onto his floor in front of him from *actual* respiratory distress.

"The fact of the matter is that your parents are in arrears to the tune of several times that amount—nearly twelve thousand dollars. Some of that is owed to me personally, although the majority is money owed to the Fifth and Third National Bank, which I own. And they told me that the majority of that debt was caused by you demanding that they spend extravagant amounts of money on you. They confessed that they'd spoiled you badly and that you demanded the best of everything, even to the point of refusing to get married—despite multiple satisfactory offers —so that you could remain with them and bleed them dry."

Vinnie sat there, utterly stunned, and definitely on the

verge of fainting at what he was telling her. Her relationship with her parents had never been very good—she wasn't at all the type of daughter they'd wanted. It had turned out that she was nowhere near pretty enough to attract a really wealthy suitor, and she was entirely too intellectually curious for their own dimwitted comfort.

She practically snorted. She cost them money! That was rich, especially since she was sitting there in a gown that her maid had worked and reworked and re-re-reworked to make certain that it still covered her in some kind of decent fashion. It was bought years ago, when she was still a teenager and on the market, and she'd naturally grown almost out of it. Lavinia couldn't remember the last time she'd had new clothes. She never went to balls any longer, so there was, technically, no need. She spent most of her days with her nose in a book—usually one she'd gotten when she'd walked all the way to the library in shoes that her toes peeped out of and soles that were so worn, they were practically non-existent.

In contrast, both her mother and her father wore the latest fashions, attended only the most popular of balls and parties, ate and drank and spent with reckless abandon, and did so with little thought to their grown daughter who remained at home alone, with only the servants for company because she'd disappointed them so utterly.

But she didn't want to say any of that to him—even in her own defense. She was much too embarrassed, in the first place, and in the second place, she stubbornly felt no obligation to explain anything to him, even if it was to her own detriment. So, Vinnie remained quiet as her mind raced, doing her best to suppress the tears that surfaced, which only served to annoy her further. They didn't deserve her tears—and she definitely included him in "they".

Meanwhile, Sterling flicked his ashes into a tray on his desk while studying her carefully as he continued to speak.

"The deal we came to was that I would forgive their debts, in exchange for your hand in marriage. Your parents told me that they had your consent to arrange such a bargain, but they warned me that you might well come to me to plead against the marriage, hoping to get even more out of me."

She could feel her face blanch white, and she clutched the arm of the chair as she began to see stars and red at the same time.

How could they have done that? Did they hate her that much? Apparently so.

"That—that's a lie. It's all lies. I didn't know anything about any of this until night before last," she replied staunchly, but she could see in his face that he didn't believe her—that nothing she said was going to change his mind. She might have said more if he'd looked at all receptive to it, but instead, she squared her shoulders and said as little as she could. "I have no idea why they were intimating that I was in on this… affront, which I most distinctly wasn't." Vinnie paused, swallowing hard. "I have no interest in marrying you or anyone else, milord." She looked down at the small, plain reticule where it lay in her lap, sniffing a bit, to her own horror, feeling more overwhelmed than she ever had in her life. "I confess that I am at a loss." Her shoulders slumped and she bit her lip, desperately holding back the tears that were threatening.

"Don't bother to cry," he warned harshly, sounding impatient. "I'm not going to give anyone in your family any more money—especially you—and I don't care how hard you sob."

Vinnie stiffened her spine at that pronouncement. She'd been determined not to marry him when she came in here, but she'd given him the benefit of the doubt that he was an honorable man who hadn't known that she wasn't aware of what her parents were doing and would have immediately let her out of the arrangement once he found out.

The reality of the situation was very hard to come to grips with, but she knew one thing: she didn't care if she and her parents ended up living on the streets, there was no way she was going to marry this man.

She was already considered a spinster—since she'd reached the ripe old age of twenty-two while remaining unmarried—and she intended to die in the same state, even from the gutter.

She'd seen what her mother had been put through by her father—and vice versa—and wasn't about to let herself fall into the same trap, just because it was what was expected of her. Vinnie had really thought that her parents had accepted her decision to remain unmarried, after long and frequent arguments about her coming out, which she eventually did, under protest.

She'd even gone to all the balls and teas and dances, too, for quite a few years, like a good daughter, knowing it would never be enough for them.

Granted, they'd never be enough for her, either, since she had no intention of choosing any of them. She'd never once found a man that she had the faintest interest in, and she was not going to simply marry for money.

But then there was the fact that she was quite cool to any man who showed any amount of interest in her, which only seemed to make some of them even more determined to win her over. Long, silent afternoons spent in her company quickly disabused all of them of that notion. She'd also flatly turned down every man who'd asked for her hand, even those who had secured her father's gleefully given permission beforehand.

When she'd finally confronted them, saying that she was removing herself from the marriage market entirely, they'd responded in a manner that hadn't surprised her in the least. They ignored her, almost entirely, and the little they had spent on her—which was damned little—in order to present her season after season, was immediately withdrawn, so that they could spend it—and more that they didn't have, apparently—on themselves, instead.

Vinnie didn't think they'd bought her *anything* in the past three years at least. Even the food she ate was leftovers from their entertaining, or she was given a small portion of what was intended for the servants, not that she cared much about food, luckily.

Apparently, she'd completely underestimated the extent of their animosity toward her for taking that stance. Granted, they'd never been particularly involved with her, and she'd come to realize when she was quite young that her only value to them was in their ability to marry her off to someone rich.

The fact that their daughter had proven to be such a disappointment in the area of providing a rich son-in-law for them didn't slow their extravagant spending down in the least. They continued to live well beyond their means, while their painfully thin daughter lived in rags.

But she rarely complained, and when she did, it wasn't for herself, but rather for a few of the servants, who were frequently owed back pay—sometimes years' worth of it— but who continued to take care of her as if she was one of their own.

For herself, Vinnie was quite happy to live the quiet, secluded, consciously inexpensive life she'd created for herself, as long as she had books to read that would help her escape her circumstances, as well as the servants, several of whom had become like family to her.

The fact that her parents had poisoned his lordship's mind about her should have been a matter of complete indifference to her because, if anything, it hardened her stance about marrying him, but she was more thrown by that news than she wanted to be. It was hard to hear that one's parents would lie so blatantly while selling their only daughter to a stranger.

It was as if they wanted him to have her, but they wanted him to hate her, too.

Vinnie took a deep breath and stood, her head down for a long moment before she brought her crystal-clear eyes to his. "Thank you for your time, sir, but I will not be marrying you."

Sterling sat there for a moment looking up at her, forgetting his manners at her strange pronouncement, but before she reached the door, he rose. "I told you that I'm not going to give you another penny," he reiterated sharply.

Vinnie stopped, her hand on the knob as she turned back to him, saying with a sharp edge to her tone, "I don't recall asking you for a penny, milord, nor anything else, for that matter. Good day."

It was in his head to chase her down—to grab her and prevent her from leaving. He wanted to start out on the right foot with her, and she was going to learn the hard way that he wouldn't tolerate her misbehaving, whether it was having a snide tone while speaking to him or trying to spend him out of house or home or trying to wheedle and cajole her way out of a punishment or into a new hat or dress.

But he let her go, since he technically had no legal right to restrain her. They were to be married in a matter of days, and then she would immediately begin to learn that he was going to keep her on a very short chain. A very short train indeed.

Vinnie couldn't get away from that man fast enough. When she got down to the bottom of the steps of his surprisingly modest office building, she wished she had enough money on her to get into a cab. "On her"—hell—she just wished she had enough money to take a cab at all, even if it was just to a home where she'd never felt welcomed or loved.

But she didn't. And, in a sudden change of plans, she turned and began to walk down the blustery street, gathering her threadbare wrap around her against the chill, unaware of the fact that the man she'd just left was watching her do so, wondering at her unusual choice.

She hadn't even tried to hail a cab, and he wondered why, if she was such a spendthrift. She'd also turned in the opposite direction of her home. Her behavior didn't fit with the picture her parent had painted of her to him, but then, perhaps she just wanted to stretch her legs a bit and get some air.

Sterling forced himself to move away from the window and sit back down behind his desk to take up the latest problem with a recent investment he'd made. He was uncomfortably close to obsessed with that woman, and he refused to allow her to take up any more of his valuable time.

Chapter 2

"WHERE IS SHE?" he bellowed.

Her father—whom Sterling had already found to be severely useless—started at his volume and the fact that the big man had practically bumped the older man's nose with his.

But his wife didn't cringe. She was the real brains of the two.

Instead, she came over to press her overtly displayed bosom against his arm, squeezing his bicep as she wound her arm through his in such a familiar manner that a third party might have thought that she was the one who was set to marry him. "Oh, I'm sure she's around somewhere. I've sent the servants to find her."

They were supposed to be married in an hour, and he seemed to be the only one who was concerned about the fact that the bride was apparently missing.

He'd dropped by a few days ago to see his intended, but, although he had been warmly greeted by her parents, Zadie Montclaire had insisted that her daughter wasn't feeling well, and thus, wouldn't be coming down from her bedroom.

That memory prompted him to turn and ask Alexander Montclaire—rather than the woman who was clinging to him with an almost obscene eagerness, "When was the last time you saw your daughter, sir?"

He seemed flustered—not that that was particularly unusual behavior, he was discovering. "Oh, I'd say it's been… a while, m'lord," he finished lamely.

"A while?" Sterling repeated with incredulity.

"She was here not long ago, I'm sure. She's always here, underfoot," his wife contributed absently, telling him just about as much as her husband had.

Patience had never been his strong suit. Certain he wasn't going to get anything of substance from these two, Sterling left the morning room to confront the butler, who was standing in the foyer.

"Ashby, when was the last time you saw Miss Lavinia?"

To his horror, the man had to think. "Well, sir, I would say it's been several days."

"Several days." Sterling could not believe what he was hearing. Then he demanded, "Take me to her room."

"Sir?" The staid butler looked apoplectic.

"Take me to her room, man. Now."

He knew it was a highly unorthodox request, but he wasn't one to let convention dictate his behavior, necessarily.

The older man did as he asked, however reluctantly.

It was a surprising distance from the front door to her room, and when he stood in it, he might have thought that it was a maid's room, it was so small and shabbily appointed. He'd been in other parts of the house, and they were quite sumptuously decorated. He wondered why her room was so drab and tucked away. It was the kind of room into which one installed one's cranky, visiting aunt, hoping that it would encourage her to limit her stay. And it was utterly empty. He checked the closet, too. Nothing.

Her parents arrived—late, as usual—to stand outside and peer into the room, as if they couldn't bring themselves to actually enter it.

Sterling's jaw set, and he made his way back into the hallway.

"I can explain, m'lord!" Zadie assured him, clinging to him like a particularly hefty limpet as he headed for the front door, not bothering to adjust his strides to those of the woman beside him as he detached himself from her as if she was a particularly odious barnacle.

"I suggest you do so, Madame," he used the term lightly in referring to her, "and quickly, before I demand my money back!"

His tone and his words inspired waterworks, of course, or whatever histrionics passed for them in this household. "We haven't seen or heard from her in days!" she crocodile-cried into an ornate lace hanky. "Since Monday afternoon! We're so terribly worried!"

That was when Vinnie had come to his office.

"So you've contacted the police?" he asked, looking from one to the other of them when neither seemed interested in answering.

"No, we wanted to see if she returned on her own."

"And no one has seen or heard from her in nearly five days?" He didn't wait for them to give him some inane response, running his hand through his hair in order to keep himself from throttling the both of them. "She could be dead by now!" Sterling headed toward the door as he shrugged into his coat, then he turned back and said, "You two had better hope I can find her, or I will squeeze my money out of you any way I can!"

When he got back into his carriage—much sooner than he had intended to, since he was supposed to be getting married about now—he told the driver to take him to

Benjamin Meyer's place on Beacon Street.

When he got to his friend's place—unexpectedly—he was shown into the man's study.

"What can I do for you..." Ben stopped right there, as Sterling was pacing back and forth, looking as if he was about to explode. "...tell me what's going on," he said quietly while pouring a stiff drink, which he pressed into the older man's hand.

It was gone in one gulp, immediately refilled, then refilled again.

Ben stopped there, though, lest he not be able to give voice to what the problem was.

"I need you to find someone."

"Glad to." He grabbed a quill and a piece of paper. "Who am I looking for?"

"Lavinnia Montclaire. My..." The word he wanted to use didn't really fit, but he couldn't think of another socially acceptable one. "...my fiancée."

Benjamin looked up at him in complete surprise. "Your—"

"Fiancée. Yes."

After giving him a description, and telling him—not once but twice—that he wanted to kept apprised of the hunt for her every step of the way, he got back into his cab, even as his friend tried to convince him to stay and have some dinner, or at least talk more about what was going on. Of course, Ben was dying to hear how he'd ended up finding himself someone to marry, when no woman he'd met— whether accidentally or more likely in a manner contrived by either the woman's nearest relative or by the woman herself —had ever seemed to measure up to his exacting standards. He'd also gone the unusual route of impressing on his friend that he was to spare no expense in finding her, which only made the mystery muddier.

Sterling was not the kind of man to throw around money for any reason, and he was amazed that the other man hadn't simply let the girl go rather than go to all of this bother.

Unfortunately for him, the man obviously didn't want to talk about any of it, even to his best friend.

He spent the ride back to his townhouse seething with anger and not a small amount of worry, which he immediately converted into even more anger.

He wasn't at all sure what it was about this woman, but he had to have her. He'd never reacted to any female in the way he did to her—and he hadn't even met her when it had begun—and he didn't like it, not one bit. He'd dodged the marriage bullet quite skillfully himself, but then it was much less of a necessity for a young man to marry than a young woman.

That was until, some weeks back, he'd personally confronted Mr. and Mrs. Montclaire in regards to the enormous sum of money they owed him, after firing the man who handled their accounts and had allowed them to rack up such debt with no collateral beyond a house that couldn't begin to cover it.

Mrs. Montclaire had immediately attempted to distract him from his purpose, first with herself—right in front of her husband—and when he showed less than no interest, she remarked on the fact that he wasn't wearing a wedding ring, and instead brought out several pictures that she said were of her daughter when she was a year or two younger, mentioning that she was available. She also hinted—much less than subtly—that the young woman was most certainly pure.

Sterling had had eligible women thrown at him—and who had thrown themselves at him, widows old enough to be his mother or grandmother—since he was fifteen because of his family's money, and no one had ever much piqued interest. But the moment he looked at those photographs—both highly posed but with very different expressions, somehow— he was lost.

And Mrs. Montclaire was still talking as he stared at her daughter with a lust that was so overpowering, it made him feel uncomfortable. The older woman sighed, as if she was terribly put upon. "She was such a sweet, kind child. It's too bad that she's become such a spoiled brat, but what mother doesn't want to give her child everything she can? Alexander and I are quite unable to control her anymore—or her spending. She the sole reason we find ourselves nearly penniless. Not only does she buy anything that she sees and likes, but she's also turned down every offer, even from the most well off and well-bred gentlemen in the state.

"We—her parents—had so hoped to find some strong young man who would be willing to take Lavinia in hand, who would take on the responsibility of curbing her misbehavior in a manner that neither Alexander nor I have been able to do. She needs a *very* firm, very strict hand to keep her in line, that one."

Those pictures and his very visceral response to them, as well as what Mrs. Montclaire was saying were more than enough to get him rock hard. So much so that he wished he had a pillow or something that he could put on his lap. Instead, he improvised with the pictures, although they perched on the bulge of his cock rather than covering it, he was afraid.

He didn't know what she knew about him—or if, God forbid—she told every suitor who came to call this very risqué spiel—but she was saying everything that he wanted to hear. If he ever got married, Sterling knew he wouldn't hesitate to subject his wife to whatever form of discipline he deemed necessary, based on whatever her misdeed was. But to find a young woman who was so obviously in desperate need of correction—it was an opportunity he would be hard put to pass up.

Sterling had held up the pictures again, staring at the woman portrayed in them. She wasn't a beauty, but then, he'd never found that necessary in order to find a woman desirable. She had something that attracted him, whether he wanted to be or not, and even though he definitely wasn't a fan of being impetuous or going off halfcocked, he nevertheless found himself negotiating with the very people he had come to personally evict based solely on a compulsive need he felt for this young woman whom he found he could neither ignore or deny.

When he arrived home, he threw his coat at his butler—Cutler—and headed for his own study to continue feeding his anger where Ben had left off—with a glass of whiskey that was damned near full to the brim.

As he sank down into the chair behind his desk, he rubbed his hand over his forehead, then down his face.

What the hell had he gotten himself into with this quickie marriage? Was it going to be worth all of this aggravation in order to have the undisputed ability to discipline her whenever he felt she needed to be, and, if her parents were to be believed, that was likely to be extremely often?

He couldn't find an answer to that question, having left the pictures at her parents'. And it wasn't even at the bottom of the glass—or the bottle.

The next morning, it wasn't the sunrise that awoke him, as it usually did. Instead, it was an exceedingly timid knock at his study door, where he'd apparently fallen asleep.

"Sir? There's a messenger here from Mr. Meyer."

If it had been anything else, Sterling might have been tempted to tell the man to go do a physically impossible act, but the fact that it was Ben who sent it sobered him more quickly than anything else could have.

Once he'd rearranged his clothing a bit and run his hand through his hair in lieu of a brush, he hollered, "Come."

The butler opened the door and stood aside, while a wet behind the ears young man bounded into the room like an eager puppy.

"Hello, Uncle Sterling!" Then he realized to whom he was speaking and amended it hastily to, "Good morning, my lord."

"Clarence, have you become your father's messenger boy of late?" Although it hurt his face, he managed to smile at the young man, who was probably all of thirteen years old, if that.

"Yes, sir! He gives me a penny a message, and I get to keep my tips!"

The boy's voice cracked as he spoke, but Sterling didn't remark about it. He frowned. "How are you getting around the city? You're a fast runner, as I recall, but that would be a lot of running."

"I use my bicycle, sir."

"Ah. Good idea! Maybe I should hire you myself!" He stuck out his hand, and Clarence produced a folded note.

Sterling:

According to the servants, her clothes were in her room until Monday night.

No one recalls seeing her enter or leave with anything.

No police reports, no one matching her description in the hospital.

Just an update. I'm still on the case. More when I have it.

Benjamin

. . .

Sterling wrote a short response, thanking his friend for his efforts and reminding him to keep track of how much he owed him. Then he gave it to Clarence, who was his godson, along with a fifty-cent piece.

"Wow! Thank you, Uncle Sterling!" The boy looked at the coin in his palm as if it was all the money in the world. And it probably was, as far as he was concerned.

"You're welcome, son. You work hard for your father or anyone else who hires you, and there's no telling how far you can go."

"Thanks! I will."

He left, and Sterling yawned loudly then headed upstairs to dress, although his normally focused mind kept drifting frequently to Lavinia. Ben knew his stuff, and as much as he wanted to help find her, he knew he'd just get in the way. He was extremely worried about her, alone in the city, assuming she'd not wandered far. Sterling frowned deeply. He hoped she hadn't, anyway. She was due a very serious spanking for putting him through, this once she was found—no doubt about it.

He refused to think about the various violent ends she might have come to that floated through his mind and distracted him for the rest of the day.

For the second time, he was awakened from by a loud rap on the door—not his favorite way to greet the day.

"What the fuck do you want, Cutler?" he screamed, unrepentant about using foul language when speaking to his servant. Cutler was most certainly used to it by now. "And what the hell time is it, anyway?"

"It's two-thirty, sir. And Mr. Meyers is waiting in the foyer."

When he heard that it was Ben, Sterling threw the covers

off and bounded out of bed. He slept in the nude, so as he pulled on a pair of pajama bottoms and threw on a robe, he said, "Show him into my study and pour him a drink. I'll be right down."

When he walked into the room, Ben was taking a sip of his drink.

"You do realize that you're taking your life in your hands waking me up in the middle of the night like this?" he threatened idly, heading to the bar to get his own generous four finger pour.

Ben didn't look worried in the least. "Even if I've found her?"

Sterling put down the drink that had been halfway to his lips. "You did?"

"Yes. She's in a boarding house in White Chapel."

He frowned. That was a notoriously bad part of town. What the hell was she doing there?

"That's not good," Sterling grimaced, already heading for the door. He stopped halfway there and turned to his friend. "Thank you for finding her—and so quickly."

"I guessed that she was pretty important to you."

Sterling was surprised to find himself nodding at the other man's words, even though they weren't wrong, exactly.

"Where are you going?" Ben asked.

"To get her, of course."

"Are you sure you want to do that? If she doesn't want to marry you—"

Ben had never seen his friend look quite as determined as he did at that moment, and that was saying something.

"I don't care whether she wants to marry me. She's going to, one way or the other." He took another step toward the door then turned around again. "Would you do me a favor?"

"Sure."

"I know it's the middle of the night, and Patience must

not be too happy with you gallivanting all over town on my behalf."

Ben snorted. "It's all right. She loves you, and she's very happy at the idea that you've finally found love."

Sterling's expression was rueful. "Well, I don't know that I've found love as much as lust, to be completely honest."

Ben gave him a knowing grin. "I don't think I'll tell her that."

"Please don't. I am honored by her affection, and I wouldn't want her to think any less of me because I'm marrying for that venal reason rather than the loftier one I'm sure she would prefer." He paused then continued. "Would you wake up Judge McCrory for me? He won't be happy, but he's always had a soft spot for me—especially since I lent him the money to start that charity of his. And wait there for me, please, if you would be so kind. I'm going to need a witness."

Ben nodded, but Sterling was already bounding toward the stairs, his long legs allowing him to take them two and three at a time.

They left his house together a few moments later, but went in opposite directions. If he hadn't known Sterling so well—knew that he could take care of himself in any situation—he might have worried about him going into that part of town at this time of night.

But if anything, it was whoever the fool was who made the mistake of confronting him who needed to be afraid, not Lord Glastonbury.

As he dismounted in front of the establishment where his runaway fiancée had stashed herself, his foreboding expression alone would be more than enough to dissuade anyone from trying to get the better of him. He looked as if he'd just come from killing someone or was on his way to do so at the moment. Either way, he was utterly unapproachable.

He knocked loudly, not caring who he woke up in the

process. Luckily, the proprietress of the establishment lived on the ground floor of the dilapidated building, and she made it to the door in record time.

Sterling didn't bother to make any kind of explanations. He simply pushed past the old woman, knowing that Vinnie was on the fourth floor, and heading up those stairs even more quickly than he had the ones in his house.

Number six was at the very back of a hall that was dirty beyond belief and stunk to high Heaven. He couldn't wait to get her out of here. No matter what she'd done, how much of a spoiled rotten brat she was, or how annoying it was that she'd done this, probably just to eek something more out of him, she didn't deserve to even know that this kind of place existed, much less live in it herself.

Without knocking, he tried the door, finding it locked. Only then, did he begin to pound on it. "Lavinia! Open this door immediately!"

On the other side, Vinnie—who was well aware of what kind of area this was and was quite concerned about her own safety and hadn't slept a wink in several days—had finally fallen into a deep sleep as her body tried to recover some of that lost shut eye. She hadn't heard the commotion downstairs and didn't start awake until someone began to bang on her door fit to bring the whole house down.

"Vinnie! Open the door this instant, or you will wish you had, I promise you!"

She rose, pulling on her robe and cinching it tightly at the waist, as if that was going to protect her from him. She had a feeling that there was little on God's green Earth that was going to be able to do that.

He continued to beat on the door until she opened it. Mrs. Dubcek, the owner of the building, was standing there next to him, not looking very happy at the commotion he was causing at this time of night and obviously blaming her for it.

The majority of her neighbors had been jarred awake by his unseemly display, too, and were peering fearfully out their doors at them.

She chose to address her landlady first, since she represented her ability to remain here. "I'm so sorry for all of the hullabaloo, Mrs. Dubcek. It won't happen again, I promise."

"Damn straight, it won't. I want you out of here tomorrow morning."

Vinnie bit her lip as she stood there in her nightgown and robe, fighting back tears yet again. This was the cheapest place she could find, and she didn't want to have to spend another day walking the streets, trying to find another rooming house she could afford.

"She'll be out of here in the next few minutes, Madame," Sterling growled, not looking at the old lady, but rather at the woman he intended to make his wife in very short order, if only to keep her from disappearing on him again. Without taking his eyes off of Vinnie, he dug into his pocket and peeled off a ten-dollar bill. "I assume this will cover anything Miss Montclaire might owe you in the way of room or board?"

As he expected, it was snatched out of his hand before he had a chance to reconsider the extravagant amount, considering she only paid twenty-five cents a night for the room— no board.

Mrs. Dubcek did her best to remained unimpressed however, sniffing indignantly, then heading back down the stairs.

Although she had no great liking for the woman, Vinnie had to stop herself from begging her to stay. She'd rather endure her irascible company than Lord Glastonbury's, any day.

But Vinnie didn't want to give him the impression that she was some kind of push over, so as soon as Mrs. Dubcek was gone, she forced herself to confront him.

"What are you doing here, milord?" she asked, proud of how calm and neutral her voice sounded, despite the way he was looking at her and how vulnerable she felt to be standing there in front of him in her bedclothes.

"What do you *think* I'm doing, Vinnie?" She didn't know him at all, but she could definitely see—and hear—that he was very close to the end of his rope. "We were supposed to get married on Friday."

She gave him a blank look that did nothing to help his temper, nor did her aloof, off putting demeanor in general. Her brows were drawn over a delicate nose. "Was I not explicit enough when I told you that I had no intention of marrying you? I think I said something to that effect at least twice." Then she pushed it further than she should have, and she knew that as soon as the sarcastic words left her lips. "Was I not speaking loudly enough?" Her tone became obsequiously solicitous. "Oh, dear. Are you hard of hearing?"

Why was she standing so close to him? she wondered belatedly, not that she thought that standing across the room would have been any better, really, but at least he would have had a harder time doing what he did as soon as she stopped speaking.

Vinnie immediately found her wrist manacled firmly by one of his hands. He wasn't hurting her, but even as she began to struggle against his hold, she knew there was no way she was going to get freed.

Not that it stopped her, especially when he took the two short steps necessary for him to get to the edge of her bed, dragging her behind him while he did so.

Before she realized his intention, she was already over his lap—the skirt of her nightgown bunched up to her waist and embarrassingly ragged bloomers pushed to her ankles—her lower half utterly bare to his gaze. And she would have sworn that—in the depths of her embarrassment—she could *feel* him looking at her. But not for long.

With no preamble, whatsoever, he began to spank her. The loud cracking rhythm of his palm on her cheeks echoed in the sparsely furnished room, and she knew that everyone on this floor—possibly in the entire building—knew what was happening to her.

Vinnie couldn't dwell on that mortifying thought or, indeed, any others involved in his little midnight visit. No, the only thing she could think of, such as it was, was when he was going to stop spanking her?

She'd never been spanked. That would have meant that her parents would have had to pay attention to her—to care enough to correct her. When she was younger, she had occasionally wished that they might, just so she would have some sign that she was more than a burden to them whom they were being forced to spend money and time on that they would much rather have spent on themselves. But the harsh reality of what she was experiencing at the moment had disabused her of that fanciful notion immediately.

To her horror, it was a very short amount of time before she got to the point where she would have done pretty much anything to get him to stop, which he showed no signs of doing. She tried not to weep and wail, but there came a point—again, embarrassingly quickly—when she could no longer do that, and she had no choice but to give full throated voice to her sounds of anguish, as well as protestations that she cringed at giving voice to, but did so nevertheless.

"Ow! Ow! That hurts! Stop! Please! My lord! *Stop! Please!*"

He ignored her completely, along with her attempts to get away, which were feeble at best and easily dealt with, especially once he'd neutralized her arms entirely by holding them together in his free hand, well up her back.

"Oh, ow! No! Stop!"

She wanted to be stoic. She wanted to simply endure what he was doing, like a martyr, with her mouth shut through the whole thing, never uttering so much as a whimper. But he made that absolutely impossible, right from the start. It wasn't until she was quite certain that she was going to die over his lap that he began to scold her at the same time, which somehow managed to make the spanking much worse.

"I can spank you like this until the break of dawn with no adverse effects to my person, you know, young lady."

She hadn't been called that in her life, she didn't think, and she certainly didn't like hearing it now.

"I do not appreciate you disappearing on me. I never told you that I was going to let you out of the bargain your parents made with me, and I wouldn't have, because they already have my money. I had no idea you'd go to this extent to avoid your responsibilities, although I guess I shouldn't have been surprised, considering what they've already told me about how selfishly you behave. You owe me, and I will have you. Be happy I'm marrying you and not just taking you without benefit of clergy!"

That would have given her reason for pause, in another situation.

"As such, I do not appreciate your sarcastic tone, Lavinia, especially since I have spent the past few days worried sick about you and have expended considerable time and energy in order to find you." Sterling took a breath then continued, never missing a beat as he blistered her behind, "So, as I said, you owe me, and as of this moment, you are mine, and you'd better resign yourself to that fact, or you're going to spend the rest of your life in some variant of this position. And believe me, my hand is far from the only thing that's going to come in contact with your backside at my behest, but it's probably the gentlest of them all."

She literally howled at that pronouncement, renewing her efforts to free herself but getting nowhere.

It was a surprisingly short time after he'd said that that he did stop, and she immediately struggled to get away from him, although he wouldn't allow her to go far, and she ended up in an ungainly heap at his feet, between his legs.

Vinnie rested herself carefully on her hip, so as to avoid touching her still naked behind to the rough, wooden floor.

Damn, Sterling thought, she looked a lovely picture, sitting there all submissive between his thighs. If he hadn't already been fully capable from the moment he'd first seen her photographs, that sight alone would have done it for him.

But he didn't have time to dwell on that now. He stood, and to her great surprise, turned his back on her. "Get dressed—something decent. Something nice, that you want to be married in."

She had gotten to her feet as soon as she could, but despite his command, she simply stood there, biting her lip and staring at his broad back. Something she wanted to be married in? That was rich, but she didn't have the guts necessary to get married naked.

After a quiet moment, he asked, his voice full of warning, "I don't hear you moving about. Do you require assistance?"

"No!" she practically yelled, crossing quickly to the small closet—with one eye on him—to grab the best of the three dresses she owned. There were two more, but they weren't fit to be seen in and should long since have been retired to the rag bag.

To her horror, he began moving around the place, although he scrupulously kept his back to her. "Do you have a suitcase?" He didn't wait for her to answer. "I'll pack it. I want to leave as soon as possible, and you are *never* coming back here."

Vinnie was to flustered to pay much attention to what he was saying.

"Vinnie!" he said sharply.

"Yes?"

"Where are your cases?" He'd already seen that her closet was essentially empty, and he had to wonder where she'd put all of her clothes and the trunks they must have arrived here in.

"It's under the bed."

A quick look beneath it produced a small valise, which he laid open on the bed and immediately began to put things in, but there was precious little to pack. He rifled through her drawers, pulling out what he assumed were her underthings, but there was a dearth of those, too. And what he saw of them were in a condition that he thought would have been more likely to be seen on her landlord, not a woman who bought clothes as often as she breathed—and then, only the best.

He crossed to the closet and got the three remaining dresses there, frowning as he looked at how worn they were, too.

Vinnie was wearing what had passed for her best dress for the last three or four years, although it was definitely the worse for the wear.

Sterling wadded up the dresses—if one could still call them that in their condition—and put them in her case, then she went to the closet after him and scarfed up the hangers, which she tried to take also.

He couldn't help but tease her, "I do have hangers at Dunston House, I promise you."

She colored, which he hadn't necessarily intended, and put them back, coming to stand as far away from him as she could as he looked around the place then closed the valise and faced her.

The frown was back on his face as he took her in. Why she'd chosen to bring such awful dresses with her—and where she'd stored the others—was a mystery to him, but he didn't have the time or the inclination to go into it with her at the moment.

She looked as if she was going to take any excuse to bolt from him again, so he did something to distract her. He walked over to her and held out her suitcase, which she took automatically. Most people who are offered something to hold will reach for and take it without thinking, and he used that to his advantage.

Then he bent over and picked her up, not bothering to worry about whether or not she was decently covered—he left that to her—and marched down the stairs with her in his arms.

Vinnie wasn't sure what she should do. It didn't seem prudent to try to get away from him when he was holding her on the stairs, and before she knew it, she was in his carriage.

"Stay put, or I'll make what you got in your room look like love pats, I promise you."

He went back to talk to her landlady—who was at the door, of course—asking her to let him know if she'd forgotten anything, or if there was anything else in storage for her, saying that he would have someone come fetch it tomorrow if there was.

Chapter 3

ALTHOUGH VINNIE FELT around in the darkness for another way out of the carriage, there wasn't one, and she didn't dare try to sneak out the door she'd just been put in. She did not want to endure another spanking from him ever, so she was going to have to be careful.

He joined her much too quickly for her tastes, and she switched benches, scrunching herself into the furthest corner away from him as she could, which wasn't very, as evidenced by the fact that he just had to reach out and scoop her off her seat with no strain whatsoever in doing so. She found herself sitting next to him, clamped to his side with one strong arm as if he thought she might fling the coach door open and throw herself onto the road. She was in a lot of despair, but it wasn't quite that bad—yet.

At least he didn't try to talk to her, and it was a short drive to their destination. He exited the coach then turned around and picked her up again, carrying her into someone's house this time—and a very nice place it was, too.

Again, she was held to his side by an arm that was just

shy of painful, as if he was silently warning her not to make trouble.

He seemed to know these two men well, and they—more than he—seemed to be trying to make this a jovial occasion, rather than the death of what freedoms she'd been able to carve out of life the hard way.

There was another woman in the room, but she sat quietly in a chair. She was introduced as Mrs. McCrory, the judge's wife.

"Well, are we ready?" the judge asked. He was holding a Bible out in front of him in a manner that bespoke great comfort, as if he'd performed this ceremony many times in the past.

Vinnie highly doubted that he'd ever conducted one like this, though. And she proved it by saying a very quiet "No" when she was asked if she took him for her husband, which had everyone gasping, and the band around her waist contracted until she could barely get a breath.

Sterling wanted to take her over his knee again right there and then, but he didn't want to embarrass his friends by doing so—not that she would know that.

So instead, he gave them a pat smile, saying, "Wedding jitters, I promise. I'm just going to have a chat with Vinnie for a moment. We'll only be a second."

He hauled her to a darkened corner of the large room, where they did have a modicum of privacy, to bend down and hiss angrily into her ear, "Is your ass not still stinging? Because I can arrange that it will—a lot more—and right in front of these very nice people."

Vinnie's eyes widened, and she gasped, "You wouldn't!"

He drew himself to his full height. "You don't know me at all, Lavinia, and I would say that is to your distinct disadvantage at the moment."

"B-but I can't! I don't love you! I don't want to marry anyone!"

Sterling sighed, then he bent down to whisper in her ear —not trusting that those in the room wouldn't have heard him if he'd given full throat to what he intended to say, although this time, he took a different tack. "Do you want to end up on the streets? Do you want your parents to end up there, too—penniless, their household dissolved, friendless, reduced to begging on the street beside you?"

She managed not to point out to him that he was at a disadvantage in not knowing her. She didn't give a whit what happened to her parents anymore or, for that matter, much about what happened to herself. There were friends she could have gone to, although she hadn't wanted to impose on them. And if her parents were also penniless, she knew they wouldn't hesitate to try to ride her coattails and prey on their sympathies in order to secure their own space with whatever friend from whom she'd decided to beg a favor.

But one line he said did catch her attention, and she paused for a second before repeating something she hadn't thought of during her little rebellion. "The household will be dissolved?"

"Of course, it will!" he hissed. "I want you as my wife, and I won't hesitate to take everything from them."

Vinnie bent her head, tears filling her eyes that she refused to allow to spill over.

Her sigh was a quiet, resigned one before she lifted her head again to meet his eyes. "I will marry you on one condition."

Sterling resisted the urge to guffaw at that, not wanting to draw anyone's attention to them. "I rather think that you're not in any kind of position to ask for conditions, my girl."

"I'm well aware that is what you think, sir." Her words weren't delivered with any amount of sarcasm or sass that he could detect. Instead, they were neutral and emotionless. The thought ran through his mind that he might prefer her sharp sarcasm to a tone that was so lacking in feeling, but he dismissed that as a ridiculous flight of fancy.

"And yet I'm going to have the audacity to ask anyway, even though I am fully aware of your low opinion of me— although I have to wonder why it is that you want to marry one such as myself."

He gritted his teeth at that, recognizing that she was not wrong. If pressed, he wasn't at all sure that he could come up with a valid reason why he had to have her. He just did.

"If you grant me this boon, I will marry you willingly."

That caught his attention as little else could have. "Yes?"

"Yes." Vinnie nodded slowly.

He liked the sound of that a lot! But what could the cost be? A fur? A Grand Tour? A yacht? He was almost afraid to find out.

And what she asked for left him confused to the point of speechlessness for a long moment.

"I would like to take three servants from my parents' household with me—my maid, Dennis, Kincaid, the groom, and George, the footman, and I'd like your word that you will employ them in perpetuity, until *they* decide to leave." They had all been exceedingly nice to her, and she didn't like the idea of leaving them with her parents. If things didn't work out between them, and she thought they might not, she might need to make a quick escape, and she didn't want to have to worry about them. She wouldn't put it past him in the least to ruin her parents even years from now.

Sterling was baffled by her request. Servants? She was asking that he take care of her servants—not her parents— but a groom, a footman, and a maid. It made no sense at all to him.

Vinnie looked up at him, but he wasn't saying anything,

and she became a bit defensive. "I don't think that's too much to ask, considering that I'm allowing myself to be sold off like so much chattel."

He refrained from reminding her that she was damned expensive chattel. When he spoke, he sounded distracted, but he said what she wanted to hear, so she didn't question it. "I'll make the necessary arrangements tomorrow."

"Thank you."

With that, she left him in the corner and headed back to the triumvirate who had been waiting patiently for them.

Her smile was one of feigned soft embarrassment when she reached them. "He was right. Just an attack of bridal nerves."

Mrs. McCrory actually hugged her, confessing that she, too, had had her own doubts about her husband of three decades. "In fact, I still do." She grinned, poking him in the ribs with a well-placed elbow.

"Adelaide! Behave!" the judge cautioned, but his eyes were full of obvious merriment and love for his wife, as hers were for him.

It was hard for her to see the two of them like that, frankly. It would have been much easier to marry this stranger by her side if the other couple in the room was a bickering mess, like her parents. But they were just showing her—tantalizing her, teasing her—with what she would now never have and had wanted for so long, a loving, romantic relationship with her spouse. Still, when the time came again, she said what was required of her.

Sterling, who couldn't seem to help but notice everything about her, already recognized the quietly defeated tone with which she recited her vows.

He'd bought her a ring, but didn't have it on him, so he took off his signet ring, which he wore on the pinky of his right hand, and put it on her finger. It was too big, of course, but there was nothing that could be done about it at the moment.

Finally, Sterling was told to kiss his wife, and aware that there were interested eyes and ears on the both of them, gave her a gentle peck on the cheek.

Of course, Ben wasn't about to let him get away with that. "Go on, man, kiss her properly! She's your wife, not your mother-in-law!"

Sterling glared at Ben but allowed himself to be teased into kissing her properly. At least, he was kissing her the way he wanted her to kiss him, but there was absolutely no reciprocation on her part. She didn't object in the least as he gathered her into his arms and pressed his lips to hers, but she didn't participate—even in the slightest way —either.

Congratulations were given and received all around, and everyone shared a glass of champagne. While Sterling thanked the two of them profusely for their efforts on his behalf and he tried to pay the judge, who looked offended at the attempt, Mrs. McCrory approached the new bride, where she had drifted away to look out the big bow window at the front of the parlor.

"I don't wish to incur any bad luck, but I saw how big his ring is on your finger, and I'm a bit worried that you're going to lose it before you have a chance to replace it with a more suitable one. If you'll give it to me, I'd be glad to do a temporary fix, anyway, until he gets you another."

When Vinnie raised her head, the other woman could see that she was on the verge of tears. She wanted to comfort her but didn't want to be overly familiar with someone she'd just met. "I'll only be a minute, my dear," she said, leaving for parts unknown with a wedding ring that she had no idea Lavinia couldn't care less about.

As she continued to stare out the window, bolting back

the last of the champagne in her glass, she found it removed from her hand.

"I think you've had enough. Your parents mentioned that to me, too—that you have a bit of a fondness for the grape."

It was on the tip of her tongue to contradict him—to defend herself—but then she decided that she didn't care to. It was over and done. Her life was ruined, and she was forever attached to a man her parents had made sure thought the worst of her.

It didn't make sense to her to keep antagonizing him. They'd gotten to him first, and he'd likely never believe what she said anyway. She'd never been much fond of beating her head against a rock.

So, she tried to move slowly away from him, but his arm slid casually around her waist in a gesture that anyone who knew they were now newlyweds—except, perhaps, the woman who was now his wife, who he had to corral into standing close to him—would interpret as loving and affectionate.

Mrs. McCrory certainly did when she returned with her ring. "Aw, it's lovely to see such an affectionate couple."

Vinnie refrained from asking her if she needed to get her eyes checked.

"There you go, dear. Like I said, it's only temporary, but at least you won't lose it tonight. Newly married women like to feel married, and the ring is a big part of that, at first," she explained to Vinnie's husband.

"I bet that's true for some of them anyway," Lavinia murmured under her breath, but not far enough, apparently, since that band of steel contracted painfully around her middle for a moment before loosening but not much.

Only a few minutes later, Sterling got everyone's attention. "My wife and I want to sincerely thank all of you for giving up your sleep for us. We are very appreciative, but I think we're going to head back to Dunston House for the night, rather than all the way out to Arbor Hall."

Ben and Judge McCrory bestowed congratulatory pecks on her cheek, but Mrs. McCrory gave her a full-on hug. "If I may give you some hard-won advice about marriage, my dear, try to remember that no one's perfect. Not you, and certainly not him," she teased with a grin that Vinnie couldn't bring herself to return when she let her go. "Just remember to love each other, and everything else will work itself out, I promise."

She thanked the other woman dutifully, but she knew that nothing Mrs. McCrory had said really pertained to what was going on between Lord Glastonbury and herself.

Soon—too soon—they were alone in the carriage, on their way to… Vinnie had no idea. She'd never been to his house that she could recall. She'd only ever been to that tiny office he had downtown, for some reason. Surely, he could afford better digs—not that she would ever suggest such a thing to him.

She couldn't. Vinnie was trying valiantly to come to grips with the idea that her life in his house would be much like her life in her parents' house. She could no more ask him for anything she needed than she could them.

And she wouldn't, no badly what it was or how badly she needed it. She wasn't about to reinforce what her parents had told him about her. She'd go naked before she asked him to get her new clothes or anything else, for that matter. She'd go without. It wasn't as if she wasn't used to doing that.

It was a quiet ride, but at least he wasn't molesting her. She couldn't quite allow herself to relax—not when he was sitting so close to her. The man bothered her in more ways than she wanted him to, but she didn't know how to defend herself against it. Even freezing him out only helped to a point, she was afraid.

What she did to distract herself was recall passages she remembered from her favorite books, calling them up in her mind and reading them, after a fashion, which allowed her some relief from the tension she was feeling.

Not to mention the way her bum was burning while she was sitting on it, despite the plush seat cushions.

She was so involved in a chapter of *Great Expectations* that she hadn't realized the coach had stopped, and her husband was standing outside it, offering her his hand to her less than patiently.

Vinnie allowed herself to be brought into his house for the first time. It was the biggest foyer she'd ever been in, with a long, grand staircase that wound around the perimeter in an elegant fashion.

"Good evening, Cutler," the man who was now her husband intoned, completely missing the other man's look of distaste at the condition of his new mistress' cloak.

He was being politer to his butler than he'd ever been to her, she thought, as a depressing feeling descended over her.

Sterling knew that he should have been gentleman enough to give her at least this evening to herself, to acclimate a bit, but he had to admit to himself the bald fact that he wasn't that much of a gentleman.

Instead, he ushered her upstairs—a big hand on the small of her back, ready to catch her if she should decide to flee again. But halfway up the long staircase, he realized that she wasn't looking around furtively for a method of escape. She wasn't looking around at all. Her face was downcast, as if she found the pattern of the carpet to be mesmerizing. Whatever was beneath her feet had been given that treatment since he'd helped her out of the carriage. He supposed that she could have been trying to lull him into a false sense of security, but something in him told him that that was not what was happening.

Sterling brought her to his room. They were not going to follow the fashion and sleep apart. He wouldn't have it—especially since she'd proven herself to be a flight risk. Of course, he allowed her to enter ahead of him, which gave him time to lock the door behind them, and Sterling was thankful that she didn't seem to notice he'd done that.

From there, he crossed to his armoire, where he kept a rocks glass, into which he poured a goodly amount of whiskey from a small flask he'd been in the habit of keeping in his sock drawer. "Here. Drink this."

She looked at the alcohol he was offering and turned her nose up at it. "No, thank you."

"Did you hear a question mark at the end of my sentence? If you did, I assure you I didn't mean you to." He practically nudged her with the glass.

Vinnie stared at it for a beat, then grabbed it out of his hand and downed it with one gulp. It set fire to her windpipe on the way down in much the same way he'd set fire to her backside earlier, and she ended up doubled over, coughing and sputtering and choking.

Not that he offered any assistance. Instead, he stood there watching her like a dolt, as if she was doing something he hadn't expected her to do upon ingesting a couple of shots of liquor in one gulp. She had no idea how drunks behaved, but apparently, it wasn't like that. She'd have to remember that for future reference.

He took a generous nip from the flask himself then tucked it away again and turned to his new wife. "Well, since your maid isn't here, I suppose her duties fall to me."

Sterling came to stand directly in front of her, looking down at how small and frail she seemed to him all of a sudden. The dress she was wearing, though, was contrastingly—and distractingly—tight in areas where it should have been loose, and loose in areas where it should have been tight. It also seemed as if it was several inches shorter than it should have been, not that he kept up with the latest fashions.

He turned her around, so that her back was to him, and began to work the buttons that ran down her back loose, but it seemed as if every third button was some kind of improvisation, rather than a repeat of the former, as if she'd had to use whatever buttons she had on hand when she lost the originals. That was puzzling, but he didn't allow himself to dwell on it—that or the fact that he could practically see through her dress in some spots.

All a play to get more from him, he was sure, he thought dismissively. He didn't know where she was hiding the rest of her no doubt extensive wardrobe, but she'd obviously selected the worst of them—ill-fitting and rag tag, wanting to elicit sympathy from him in the form of a new wardrobe. But he wasn't about to allow her to manipulate him like that. He was going to keep a tight rein on her, just as her parents had recommended—just as he preferred.

He relieved her of the dress and threw it into the corner of the room. She started at that, eyes wide but still not looking at him but rather after the dress as if it was something precious to her. She went so far as to lurch toward it, although he was quick enough to catch her and keep her from going after it.

"Leave it," he ordered in a clipped tone. "And I'll reiterate. If you think that playing the little match girl is going to get you new clothes, you've got another thing coming. You'd be wise to produce the rest of your things as soon as possible, because you're not going to get so much as a pair of stockings from me until you do."

She froze at his harsh words and his accusatory tone, relaxing in his hold in a manner he wasn't expecting, no longer leaning toward the crumpled pile of rags across the room, but standing, quiet as a mouse, as if hoping he wouldn't notice her.

But she was too late for that. Much too late, especially considering that she was standing there stark naked. His body, his mind, every molecule was filled with her. He ached in so many ways—those familiar as well as tantalizingly new to him—whenever he was near her, and he longed to be at her side any time he wasn't.

Those were unfamiliar and undesirable emotions that he did his best to ignore, as they were inflicted upon him against his will. In fact, he intended to exorcise those feelings by using her freely, any time he wanted to. She was his, anyway, bought and paid for, with even so much as his freedom. He'd tied himself to her in a way that, before meeting her, had been inconceivable to him, and now, as he fingered her still too big ring, he knew it wasn't going to be enough.

None of it—nothing—would or could be. He'd lost his mind, definitely lost control, and he wasn't at all happy about the loss of either, even as the thought of taming her tantalized and tormented him relentlessly.

And here she was, standing docilely in front of him, and he intended to have her. As it was, he was dangerously close to unmanning himself—as close as he had ever been in his life.

Sterling's hands very nearly spanned her too slim waist as he lifted her and less than gently laid her on the bed, although to her it felt as if he was treating her in much the same way he'd treated her dress.

All of a sudden, he was caging her with his big body, and she wanted desperately to cringe away from him—to sink into the soft mattress and through it to the floor and then the floor below, until she was able to make good her escape.

But there would be no escape for her. Even if all of the doors between her and freedom were open, she couldn't—wouldn't—walk through them. The servants whose futures she had bargained for deserved better, considering how they had helped her over the years. Even without the bargain she'd made with the devil who was so close to her right now, she had known that she was trapped, even as she made her ill-fated attempt to flee, and was inevitably going to end up bound to him for eternity. There might as well be some good to come out of it for someone.

The man who was now her husband bent down to kiss her, his lips teasing and demanding at the same time, and in a different situation, if they had met under more normal circumstances, she might well have at least attempted to kiss him back or offered some slight form of encouragement. He obviously knew a lot about kissing, and he didn't make it easy for her to resist him—pulling a bit away and nibbling gently at her lips, outlining them with the tip of his tongue, then kissing her more gently than he had before, although still very passionately.

But she refused to allow herself to respond to him in any way.

Sterling wished he had the patience to coax her along—especially this first time. But the bald face truth was that he possessed neither the patience nor the will to do so—as much as it embarrassed him to admit it. Thus, he was unable to take the time with her as he should have.

Although there was also the unkind thought in the back of his mind that if she had been allowed to run as wild as her parents had described to him—as they found themselves unable to curb her behavior—she might not be quite as pure as he might like to think of her, so there may well be no reason for him to go slowly.

That idea soothed his nagging conscience enough to allow him to ignore the fact that the thighs he parted were obviously very reluctant to do so, although not to the point of outright defiance.

He imagined—titillated himself—with the thought that she was probably not in any hurry to earn a repeat punishment, glad that it was already proving to be a deterrent.

As Sterling reached down to guide his cock to her entrance, he teased her—but more himself—a bit by using the weeping head to part her delicate folds, running it from the top of her, over her clit, and all the way down through every bit of that very sensitive territory, then back up again to settle where it belonged, between those shy, smaller lips at the slight notch created by her opening.

Casually wondering if his new wife was still feeling the effects of the discipline she'd been subjected to earlier, he reached beneath her to squeeze a rounded cheek tightly. Her reaction confirmed that she was most definitely still uncomfortable there.

It also made her groan loudly at first—until she clamped her mouth shut—and naturally arch up, away from the rough touch of his hand. Thus, she impaled herself on his cock—halfway to the hilt—but more than enough to relieve herself of her own virginity in one utterly unknowing, completely unintended motion. A pitiful yelp escaped her lips at the pain—which was more than enough to distract her from the flames that still licked at her behind.

Well, he had been wrong about her innocence. She had definitely been intact.

He did his best to wait and give her some time to become accustomed to him, and when he moved a few minutes later, she made no other sounds. But he could feel how she tried to cringe away from him, those usually startlingly bright eyes of hers closing in a face that was tense with pain.

As much as he simply wanted to plow into her, without regard to how much it might hurt her for him to do so—and large part of him did want him to do exactly that—he instead pulled out and reached over to the drawer of his nightstand, where he took out a jar of something.

After dipping his fingers into it to come up with a generous dollop of something to replace the slickness that she wasn't producing, he resumed his previous position over her, moving his loaded fingers between her legs.

Vinnie, whose eyes had opened the moment he'd left her, wondering what new torture he was going to come up with, was already hurting considerably in that area, and she didn't even think about it. Her body took over completely and she tried to jerk away from him, although she didn't get very far, of course.

Sterling caught her eyes, murmuring in an unexpectedly gentle way, "Steady," as he held her still with one hand and applied the salve—inside and out as gently as he could—to her and then to himself.

He felt her stiffen—saw the apprehension she was feeling written plainly on her face—when the head of his cock found its way between her inner folds again, but then he watched her force herself to relax. It was as if a curtain had been drawn over her face, and it became devoid of any expression at all as her eyes closed, as if she couldn't bear to see what was being done to her.

That was when he began to push his way into her again, unable to stop himself from closing his own eyes in the bliss that the feeling of her closing so tightly around him brought to him. And although he knew the advance of his long, thick cock into her virginal passage must have been causing her a certain amount of discomfort, he heard not one word of protest, nor did she try to cringe from him again in any way, even when he sank into her to the fullest with a groan of pure pleasure that was ripped from the back of his throat.

His face was buried in the pillow, next to her head, for a long moment, until he raised himself on his hands and, somewhat against his will, began to thrust into her.

"Eyes on mine, Vinnie," he commanded, more curtly than he intended, but his needs wouldn't allow for him to temper his tone.

They sprang open, and he never once had to remind her not to close them or move them.

But he came close to wishing he hadn't asked her to do that as she stared at him, wide eyed, her otherwise blank expression taking on what he saw as an accusatory undertone that he found disconcerting.

Not that it deterred the freight train that was his desire for her in the least, but it did tickle his brain about the fact he hadn't ensured that she was as frantic for him as he was for her. He had been remiss in what he considered to be one of his most paramount duties as her husband.

There would be time enough for that, though. He would be certain to make it up to her. There was little else he loved more than seeing a woman in the throes of ecstasy that he had brought to her—especially if he had brought her there after a punishment that had her in real tears, thoroughly enjoying the challenge of guiding her from agony to ecstasy.

The idea of that contrast—and exploring it on his new wife—was what put him over, hurtling himself into the abyss of absolute, ultimate pleasure that had him crying out and spasming so hard within her, spurting great gobs of seed into her, that he thought he saw stars.

Sterling collapsed down onto her, covering her small body entirely with his big one, although she made not a peep of protest, and it was he who noticed that she was being crushed into the mattress by his weight.

"Lavinia," he panted and chided in the same breath, "you must tell me when I'm suffocating you."

Nothing. Not a word. Her eyes were still open, although no longer on his, but rather were staring at the ceiling as if it held the secret to life.

His "Answer me when I say something to you. Please," was delivered with no small amount of bite, and the 'please' was a definite afterthought.

"All right."

He found her answer less than satisfactory somehow, although there was nothing technically wrong with it. But it was as devoid of human feeling as her face had been throughout and set his teeth on edge.

There were several more things that—if he had been less exhausted—he might have said to her, but he was just too tired to go down those roads at this moment.

"Stay there. I'll be right back."

Where would I go? Vinnie asked herself but kept the question to herself.

He was back quickly with something in his hand that turned out to be a soft, folded cloth that he'd dampened.

Lavinia had closed her legs as soon as he'd rolled off her, but now he was lying beside her with the cloth in his hand, ordering—definitely not asking, "Open your legs."

She didn't want to. She *really* didn't want to. Of all of the ways in which she was being expected to submit to him, this invasion of her personal, physical privacy was the worst—the hardest to bear.

But more than that, she didn't want him to spank her

again. At some point in the near future, she knew that she wasn't going to be able to avoid further punishments. But for the moment, especially since what he was asking wasn't going to hurt her inherently, she closed her eyes and did as he said.

The cloth actually felt very good when he pressed it to her overworked, distinctly sore privates, although she emitted a small gasp that she hoped he hadn't heard, when his fingers parted her nether lips in order to get at the hidden parts so that he could thoroughly clean—and soothe—her.

"Open your eyes."

What difference did it make to him whether her eyes were closed or not? she wondered, but she dutifully complied, staring up at the ceiling with steely resolve as he ministered to her, and then to himself, before throwing the cloth in the same general direction as he had her dress.

When he'd finished, Sterling felt at a bit of a loss. He hadn't spent a lot of time imagining what being married would be like, but he had kind of assumed, he supposed, that he would have the same kind of loving relationship that his parents had had, and thus he and his new bride would have spent their first night together cuddled up in each other's arms.

His situation, though, was far from his parents', and he could hardly complain about it, since it was entirely of his own making.

But then he shrugged those fanciful feelings off. The love match that was his parents' relationship was the exception rather than the rule.

And if he wanted to feel her in his arms, even when he wasn't making love to her, then that was what was going to happen. So, he reached out and brought her against him, turning the both of them onto their sides and curling himself around her from behind.

"Sleep."

Vinnie's big mouth didn't do her any favors when she couldn't resist whispering something under her breath that he was never meant to hear.

And he didn't know what she said, but she'd said so little that he wanted to know what it was.

"What did you just say?"

"Nothing."

"Vinnie."

She rolled her eyes at the clear warning in his tone, grateful that he couldn't see her do that.

"Yes?"

"Tell me what you said."

She wouldn't have thought that she would have gotten into trouble with him again so soon, especially considering the deterrent that the first spanking really was to her.

But apparently not enough of one to curb her tongue.

Sighing, she figured that his next step was either going to be to threaten again or to just start spanking her for not responding, so she might as well just get it over with.

"I said, 'Oh, do I have your permission to close my eyes *now*?'"

It was much later before either of them got any sleep, but perhaps her second spanking of the day would teach her to keep her fat mouth shut around him.

Chapter 4

VINNIE WAS AN EARLY RISER, so just about the time the sun came up, she got out of bed as she usually did. But she certainly didn't bound out of it, although she didn't sit on the edge of it at all—as she might have—because, after her stupid last act of the night before, she felt as if her rump was going to fall off. Or not, which would be a much worse fate.

She stood there for a moment, like a fawn in the woods, waiting to see if he stirred at her movements, but he didn't, thankfully.

The first thing she did was rush to her dress. It was damp in spots from the rag he'd used to clean them last night— twice, she remembered with burning cheeks at both ends— and wrinkled but salvageable.

She'd have to wear the other one today, and it was in even worse repair.

Dressed—such as she was—she made her way downstairs to the foyer just in time to see a cart pulling up the drive, only it didn't go to the front door, but rather to what she thought was probably the servant's entrance.

On a whim, she made her way downstairs, bestowing

smiles on all of the agog servants whom she met along the way, until she found their entrance and, upon throwing open the door as they all watched in rapt curiosity, the mistress of the house ran out to greet three of their kind!

The first was a plump, older lady who was obviously her maid. The young mistress threw herself at the other woman, and they hugged like old friends.

The other two were an older and a younger man, and the servants in the downstairs hall, who were all huddled in the alcove by the door, were immediately wondering amongst themselves as to what their positions might be in the household.

But then their new mistress solved that for them. "Kincaid, I don't know what kind of arrangements have been made for you, so you'd best just come inside and we'll get you sorted out. George, you too, and I'll introduce the both of you to the butler, and I'm sure he can take it from there."

They both bowed to her, saying with great deference, "Yes, ma'am," which made her uncomfortable. She'd been so concentrated on trying to avoid this marriage, she'd forgotten that she'd become a lady in the process.

Vinnie moved to slip her arm through Dennis', but the other woman pulled back. "I've a little wedding present for you, ma'am," she beamed, taking her to the back of the cart. In it, was a large trunk.

Vinnie looked at it, and then at Dennis, then back again before it dawned on her.

"My books!" She opened the top, and there they were.

"I rescued as many as I could for you, ma'am. I don't think I got them all, but I got most."

Lavinia was beside herself with glee at seeing the stacks of them that Dennis had carefully placed in the trunk. It was like being reunited with old friends.

"George, get the trunk down and bring it up to milady's

bedroom once you've been introduced." Dennis could be a bit bossy, but only ever in defense or to the benefit of her beloved mistress. She had neither chick nor child, and her mistress was her world.

"What have we here?"

Lord Glastonbury strode out of the servants' entrance of his own London townhouse, which was something he didn't think he'd ever done before.

The men nodded and the women curtsied before him, but not even his wife said anything.

"Lavinia?" he asked, not unkindly.

"This is Dennis. She's my maid. George is a footman, and Kincaid, a groom, all come from my parents." She hoped he remembered their arrangement. She wasn't interested in getting into it here, in front of everyone.

He shook each of their hands and welcomed them to his house, saying he was sure that they would all do well here. It was a decent, respectful thing to have done when many would never have bothered, when she really didn't want to like anything about him.

"I heard something about books?"

Vinnie colored. "Yes, Dennis was kind enough to bring my books—well, most of them anyway—from my parents' house."

"I would think the more important question was whether or not she brought you any clothes." Sterling stood in front of her, looking her up and down. "That dress is even worse than the one you were wearing yesterday, Vinnie. You and I will have a discussion about this later."

He tipped up her chin and bent down to brush his lips against hers. "For the moment, I have things to attend to in town, but I will be home for dinner."

And with that, he was gone, and she could breathe again,

sort of, what with the sword of Damocles hanging over her head about their "discussion".

He had always dressed for dinner, and he was in the drawing room waiting for her promptly at eight. Actually, he'd been there since seven thirty, awaiting her arrival much more eagerly than he wanted to admit. The grandfather clock tolled eight, but she wasn't there.

Sterling sighed and called Cutler in to him. "Did you let her maid know when she was expected for dinner?" he asked.

"Yes, m'lord."

"Thank you. That will be all."

He had just put his drink down and was heading for the door to go upstairs and bring her down there—after applying a generous dose of discipline that would help her remember to be on time—when the door opened and she came in.

She might have been a terrible brat, but he could tell, somehow, that she had no idea how lovely she was, even in the horrible dresses she insisted on wearing. And this one was the worst yet. It looked like something that a governess in a declining household would wear—solid drab green, service-able cloth, and uninspired cut.

But, contrarily, the simplicity of her clothing only seemed to make her stand out. Her hair was up in a beautiful chignon, with curling tendrils about her ears and in the back. She was wearing no makeup—but then she didn't really need any—and only the slightest hint of rosewater as a scent, which seemed perfect for her, to his mind. In each ear, was a small teardrop earring—diamonds, if he didn't miss his guess —and they completed her very understated, to say the least, ensemble. And she looked more gorgeous to him than if she'd been in the most expensive outfit and jewels money could buy.

She saved her hide from another spanking by saying immediately, and with unselfconscious charm, "I'm sorry I'm late, sir. I was reading and lost track of time."

He came to stand in front of her, and Vinnie could feel him appraising her, automatically bracing for his inevitable criticism.

But he surprised her by saying in a deep, honest tone that she wished didn't make her feel as all over warm as it did, "You look lovely, Vinnie. But don't be late for dinner. I won't wait for you, and you won't like the consequences if I have to go in without you."

Then he offered her his arm, and she tucked her hand into the crook of his elbow with such genuine tentativeness that it tugged at his heart. She stood very small next to him, and he experienced a sharp flash of desire when he remembered how her body felt when it enveloped and held him in such a tight, intimate embrace.

That thought made him want to take clear the enormous mahogany table of the expensive china and silver it had been laid with, sending it crashing to the floor in favor of lifting her on to it and making a meal of her. He wanted to hear her screams of unbridled ecstasy echoing around the room. But he reined himself in—finding it alarmingly hard to do so —and reminded himself that it would be all the sweeter to have her if he waited a bit. Still, he was forced to clear his throat and give his head a small shake. What was this woman doing to him? He was thinking like a lovesick boy sometimes.

Instead of leaving it to Cutler, he seated her himself at one end of the table, then himself at the other. It was big enough to hold twenty, so they were quite some ways apart, and after the first course was served, he made the unusual move of picking up his service and bringing everything down to her end, setting himself up again on her right.

"It's ridiculous for us to shout at each other, I think," he explained, taking his seat. "And besides, I can't see you without using binoculars, and not being able to see one's beautiful wife when one looks up from one's plate is a terrible tragedy."

He loved how her cheeks pinkened naturally when he complimented her.

"Thank you," she returned softly. "You're very handsome yourself."

"I wasn't fishing for a compliment, my dear."

"I know. And I wouldn't have said it if I didn't think it was true," she stated definitively.

Despite what he knew about her tendency to lie, he was inclined to believe her.

Their dinner was surprisingly companionable. Sterling did his best to be charming and delighted her with tales of his travels. He'd spent a certain amount of time abroad in various parts of the world, and not always in the best of company. He told her about running along the rooftops in Naples with none other than Benjamin Meyers, whom she'd met last night, trying to evade the police as best they could—having started a brawl that became much larger than the original participants—until they could make their way back to their hotel.

Her eyes were wide during his stories of adventures such as she had never had and likely never would. He'd been to Africa and had seen lions and rhinos and elephants, and he'd been to America, too.

They were at the end of their meal, and he mentioned, "You and your maid were talking about books when I interrupted you this morning. I take it you read?"

She reddened again, as if she had been caught doing something she shouldn't have. "Yes, I do."

He stood, getting her chair for her, then taking her hand in his. "Then I have something I want to show you."

They went up two flights of stairs, took a left and then a right, and headed for the double doors at the end of a long hall, which he stopped and threw dramatically open. Inside, was a good-sized room lined, floor to ceiling, with books.

While she put her hands to her cheeks and walked into the room, spinning slowly around in awe, he watched her avidly, knowing she was paying absolutely no attention to him.

"It's nowhere near as big as the library at Arbor Hall, but I imagine it'll do until we get there. And if there's something you want that's not there, you can always ask the librarian at Arbor Hall—Mr. Zota—to send it to you if we have it."

"You have a library?" she sighed in reverence, still not looking at him. "*Two* libraries? *And* a librarian?"

He almost corrected her, saying, "*We* have two libraries and a librarian," but something held him back from doing so.

But he still felt an immense pleasure he hadn't been expecting at being able to make her so happy with something he'd taken for granted all his life.

She stopped whirling around and approached the shelves, treating each volume that caught her fancy as if it was priceless when she pulled it from its place. Granted, some of them were, but not all. Sterling was glad that she enjoyed reading. It gave them something in common.

And, unlike many of his sex, he liked smart women. There was absolutely no challenge in securing the submission of a woman who was an idiot, who had no awareness of what was being asked of her. It had always been his ultimate goal to find a woman who knew herself and her worth, who was his intellectual equal, but who would surrender herself to him—even if somewhat reluctantly.

Unfortunately, women like that were few and far between —or at least, they seemed that way—because they were taught to hide their intelligence lest they offend a man's delicate ego, especially an eligible man.

"Oh, you have a copy of *Jo's Boys*!"

"Do you enjoy Miss Alcott's work?"

"I do! I've taken that book out of the library so many times that they practically have it ready for me at the desk when I go in!"

"And why didn't you simply acquire a copy for yourself?" he asked in a neutral tone.

But she closed up on him anyway. "I was unable to."

Sterling never understood it, but he knew some people weren't fans of educating their daughters beyond the very basics. Shrewdly, he asked, "Did your parents not support you in your love of reading?"

His keen gaze noted that her color became high again, although her answer was offhand enough as she continued to scan the volumes in front of her. "My parents didn't care whether or not I read, or whether I did much of anything, as long as it didn't cost them money. And libraries are free."

His eyebrows went up at that tidbit of information, but he remained silent, glad she was talking with him. He indulged her a bit longer as he thoroughly enjoyed watching how animated and happy she seemed amongst the books. But, by then, his body was making demands that he intended to satisfy, and he had waited just about as long to do so as he was willing to before coming to stand in front of where she was sitting curled up with a book written by Charles Darwin. It was an unusual choice for a woman, but again, he applauded her intellectual curiosity.

Still, when he extended his hand to her, he expected her

to take it. For just the slightest second, he thought she was going to rebel—which was not necessarily something he was against. In fact, he relished the thought of taming her, if that ever happened.

But he could almost pinpoint the moment at which she exerted her own considerable will, closing the book and putting her hand in his. He only admired her that much more because he knew that she truly didn't want to obey him —marital vows and strange bargain be damned.

Sterling led her out of the library and upstairs to their room. Her maid was there, waiting for her—and probably had been since after dinner.

"Dennis, you may leave," he said quietly as soon as they entered, and she did so as he considered her intently, wondering why she looked so familiar to him—not about the face, but there was something else about her that he couldn't quite pin down.

His new bride was standing nervously in the middle of the room, and he didn't miss the exchange of sympathetic glances between Vinnie and Dennis as she left. Those looks made him feel like an ogre, but not enough to deter him from taking what he wanted from her.

But there was another matter to deal with before he brought them both to the heights of bliss. "Lavinia, please put that chair in the center of the room."

His request surprised her. She hadn't even noticed that there was a chair there, where he was pointing. But she did as he asked, not immediately discerning its purpose.

Sterling, on the other hand, had hand selected the chair and had it put there for the express purpose of using it the way it was intended—for a husband to sit on while he punished his wife.

She was standing near him as he sat down, and it was

easier than he'd thought it would have been to pull her over his knees.

He heard her "oof" once, obviously in surprise, but she was almost annoyingly quiet as he arranged her skirts—which seemed to be deceptively voluminous—up over her back, then divested her completely of bloomers that had seen much better days.

"I believe I've spoken to you before about your wardrobe, and I find it silly and childish that you refuse to wear the clothing your parents so generously bought for you. I expect you to produce that clothing tomorrow. You tell me where to find it, and I'll send a carriage for it. It's ridiculous for you to continue to wear rags when you have nicer clothes available, just because you want more and nicer clothes from me. I can assure you that you're not going to get them."

It was on the tip of her tongue to tell him the truth—her truth, the *real* truth—but she had a feeling that he wouldn't believe her anyway, and she would find it quite galling to tell him that her parents were liars and were badmouthing her and have him defend them to her, painting her as a bad daughter. And she knew beyond a shadow of a doubt that was what he would do.

So, she kept her mouth shut, even when he began to use his enormous palm to redden first one cheek, then the other, in an unrelenting rhythm that had her struggling to keep her lips clamped shut after only a few hard, unforgiving swats.

When he spoke, his tone was far from harsh, and that was almost worse for her. Harsh, she could handle—slightly wistful and shame inducing was horrid for anyone with a conscience to hear.

"Don't you want to look nice for your husband, Lavinia? Don't you want me to be proud of you, to make other men wish they were me when I have you on my arm? I'm not a penurious man, and when your current dresses need replacing—or perhaps as a birthday present or something like that—I would be glad to take you to Paris myself to buy you pretty new things for the Season."

She jerked violently every time flesh found increasingly hot, red flesh, but that was all she did.

"But I cannot condone profligate spending just because you find a pretty bauble or hat or whatever in a shop window. Do you realize that you very nearly bankrupted your parents with your willful disregard for money?"

The speed with which his hand descended quickened, making it just that much harder for her to maintain her composure, to which she was barely holding on to as it was.

The wistfulness was gone as if it had never been when he commanded harshly, "Answer me, Lavinia! I'm not talking to hear myself speak!"

She wasn't exactly sure what the question was any more —the pain was muddling her ability to think. But she hazarded a guess and answered breathlessly, "Y-yes, sir."

"Exactly. So, tomorrow morning, I want you to find me in my study and tell me where to send the footmen with the carriage, and we'll have your pretty clothes in the closet before lunch, yes?"

Vinnie hung over his legs in abject surrender as he continued to spank her.

"Yes?" he repeated more pointedly, smacking even harder and faster than before.

When she opened her mouth, Vinnie wasn't sure if it was going to be to cry out and sob piteously, or answer him with what she knew was a lie.

The "yes, sir," that came out of her mouth was soft and defeated.

The spanking ended almost immediately, but besides her agreement at the end, he wasn't sure whether he'd had much effect on her, since she'd remained abnormally still over his lap while he was punishing her, neither gasping nor moaning nor crying during its administration.

A few minutes later, he helped her off his lap, then he stood to relieve her of the rest of her clothing, leaving her hair up and her earrings in. The rest of it all ended up in the same ignominious corner as her dress had last night.

She even managed to suppress her natural tendency to want to cover her nakedness, which had her arms aching at her sides to do so.

"Well," he said, standing in front of her. "I played ladies' maid to you last night. I've already dismissed my valet, James, in favor of you assuming his role."

He had to bend down in order for her to get to his bow tie, and when she'd undone it, Vinnie wasn't at all sure what to do with it.

"Just form a neat pile on the chair. James'll take care of it in the morning."

She nodded, blushing when she wondered if James would wonder why the chair was in such an unusual position in the room, but then she busied herself by helping him off with his jacket. That was challenging, too, but he helped, and soon he was standing before her in an undershirt and shorts.

She'd never be able to take the undershirt off over his head, so he removed it himself and handed it to her. She folded it and added it to the pile, returning to him with surprising alacrity to divest him of his shorts without batting an eyelash.

Then Vinnie found herself standing before him again.

Chapter 5

SHE WAS PINK WITH EMBARRASSMENT, which he found endearing but behaving bravely, he thought, which only added to a growing admiration that he hadn't expected to find for his wife, given what he knew about her.

He had thoroughly enjoyed watching her undress him, especially when she turned away from him to put an article on the chair and he could see her well-tanned behind. There was ample evidence of just how much he loved watching her standing at attention between them, although he knew she was scrupulously avoiding looking at that area. And even when she did look at him, when she met his eyes, he had the feeling that she was looking right through him, as if he wasn't really there to her, somehow.

At the moment, she was staring straight ahead, which meant that she was looking about mid-chest on him.

His fingers tipped her head back until she had no choice but to meet his. "A very good start, Vinnie," he complimented before taking her mouth with his.

It was a different sort of a kiss from last night's, although perhaps that was just the fact that they were standing? Vinnie had never kissed anyone before, so she didn't have anything to compare him to. But it felt good—really good—much better than she wanted it to by far.

Sterling kissed her deeply and passionately, taking what he wanted from her, bending her to his will, wrapping a hard arm around her waist to bend her back over it, forcing her up on to her tiptoes with her back arched to present those high, firm breasts to their best advantage.

And he was definitely distracted by them. She had given him no overt indication whatsoever that she was involved in what was happening between them in the least, although he took heart that her nipples were firm, plump peaks as he drew each of them in turn into the wet heat of his mouth, sucking gently at first, then more firmly.

If he hadn't been looking at her, he would have missed her only response to what he was doing—when he'd covered that tight peak with his mouth for the first time, her eyes went very wide, but he could detect no other response from her.

Sterling wasn't sure whether she wasn't feeling anything, somehow, or if she was simply willing herself not to show that he was affecting her in any way.

But he intended to find something that earned him a sigh or a soft moan or something. He'd even take her trying to get away from him, although he'd subdue her immediately, of course. At least that would be some kind of a reaction, though.

Before he could do that, realistically, he had to do what he didn't usually and find satisfaction himself before he tried to guide her to it.

He didn't think he'd realized that he'd ended up lifting her off her feet while he was busily suckling at her breasts, but he set her down gently and took a small step away from her. He thought she might stumble or be a bit dizzy when he did that, but she was rock steady.

She was going to be a tough nut to crack, he could see.

Then he reached out to cup her cheek and said but one word, "Kneel."

Vinnie took a deep breath and dropped to her knees before him.

"Open your mouth, wife." It was a firm—but not angry or nasty—command.

Although she had no frame of reference for this, either, she could tell where this was going.

Seconds later, her mouth was slowly being filled with the part of him that had filled her elsewhere last night. It was a very different feeling, although not unpleasant, for the moment.

"Cover your teeth with your lips, Lavinia," he ordered in a somewhat high pitched, pained tone.

She did so immediately and could feel his entire body relax. It was a very strange experience. She simply knelt there, not really doing anything but keeping her teeth from hurting him and allowing him to use her mouth. It was harder to accommodate him later, when he was pumping more quickly and forcefully past her lips, but that didn't last very long before he cried out and something warm spurted against the back of her throat. She didn't have a choice about whether or not she was going to swallow it. It was already past that point when it happened.

He remained in her mouth, his big body shuddering several times quite violently, and she wondered if it was a sign of illness, although he seemed perfectly fine otherwise.

Eventually, he stepped back, and she sank back onto her heels, still looking anywhere but *there*.

"That was wonderful, Vinnie," he purred. "Allow me to return the favor."

She had no idea what that meant, but she wasn't being given a chance to consider it, either. Instead, he leaned down to pick her up as if she weighed nothing at all. And, having seen her naked, in the light, her husband was definitely of a mind that she needed to put on a few pounds. Maybe more than a few pounds. She was painfully thin.

He'd noticed how she'd delicately devoured everything that was presented to her during dinner last night. Every plate a footman had collected was empty, and she'd had seconds of dessert.

He'd teased her that she might get fat if she continued to eat that way, but he regretted having done so now.

So, as he laid her down on the bed on her back—with a gentleness that he could see surprised his wife—he mentioned casually, "I don't want you to skip any meals, Vinnie. I know I made a comment about you getting fat, but that was before I realized how skinny you really are. I know it's the fashion, but I think you're taking it too far. So, you are to eat all of every meal."

"Yes, sir."

He didn't think he'd ever heard her use his first name, and he missed that. He didn't mind her calling him "sir", but that was what everyone called him. He would have liked to have had the kind of relationship where she would call him Sterling, but if that wasn't to be, then it wasn't.

***

His wife wasn't thinking about that at all. She was thinking that he would never believe the reason why she was so thin.

A soon as she had stopped cooperating in the hunt for a rich husband, her parents had refused to allow her to come to the table with them, decreeing that she should eat what-ever was left from the servants' meals, which was precious little. If it hadn't been for Dennis sneaking food to her from her own plate, as well as the things Cook tried to put by for her, she didn't know what she would have done.

"What happened between us last night must have seemed very strange to you. Did you know anything about what transpires between a man and a woman before then?"

"No."

"Well, it was over and done with much too quickly, and I know that it must've hurt you, and I'm sorry for that. But it never has to hurt again."

It already did—even the silky sheets on his bed weren't soft enough to keep her well-spanked behind from hurting as she lay on it. But she didn't say that to him. She didn't say anything to him, unless he asked her a direct question.

Sterling kissed her then, in much the same way as he had before, and it felt amazing. It was very hard for her not to kiss him back, but Vinnie managed not to—just barely.

Frustrated by her lack of response, he stretched out beside her, watching her closely as he dragged his fingertips, in the barest of touches, down over her face, her neck, her collarbones, making short brush strokes with fingers that were surprisingly callused for a peer of the realm, but it still felt incredible to her. He was making every nerve she possessed stand up at attention, even though she remained utterly still as he did so, trying to marshal her will over her own body and force it to obey her instead of him.

Index and thumb captured nipples that were still hard and slightly damp from his previous attentions, plucking at them, pinching them slightly and twisting just a bit, back and forth for the longest of times, one to the other, making sure they each got equal treatment.

When he moved on, she had to suppress a sigh of relief. Surely, if he had continued doing what he had been doing, she would have broken down and moaned, arching her breast up into his hand. Or preferably his mouth.

She tried to disabuse herself of that thought, but it stubbornly remained and festered, spreading tendrils of something she didn't want to confront throughout her body, joining and reinforcing others that had already snuck by her due to his efforts. It seemed the more divorced from the situation she tried to remain, the more her body rebelled at those restrictions.

As he bent his head to make her thought come to life, he murmured softly, "Open your legs for me, Vinnie."

She wanted to disobey him in the worst way, despite what she knew would happen to her rear end. But she wasn't here to defy him. He had agreed to take care of her servants, and she would do nothing to jeopardize their futures. Hers was already a dead loss, but theirs didn't have to be.

So, she forced herself to do what, at that point, was what she least wanted to do. She exposed herself to him, splaying her legs in a manner that no decent woman would.

The thought occurred to her, however, that he was asking her to do what no decent man would, but she was so ignorant of that subject that she couldn't be sure she was right about that.

She debated within her own mind while not paying any attention to what he was doing until he covered her nipple with his mouth and her mons with his hand at the same time.

Vinnie couldn't help it. She jumped. The urge to run away was almost overwhelming. It was very strange to all of a sudden realize that a man *did* have the right to touch her there, that she no longer had sole autonomy over her body. That this man, in particular, had that very private, very intimate right to touch her anytime, anywhere he wanted to, and apparently, he believed in exercising it.

Before she knew it, every bit of that which had barely felt

her own touch was covered by his hand—the same one that had made her backside a throbbing wreck. She would swear that it was still warm from her spanking!

She swallowed down the whimper that bubbled up in her throat when one finger gently breached her folds, and it was almost worse that he was treating her so carefully. It would have been a lot easier for her to remain unaffected if he was being rough or demanding or autocratic, which she would have sworn was how he always was. But apparently, not in situations like this.

And she wasn't the only one who was making revealing discoveries about their spouse. As soon as his middle finger parted her lips, it was drenched by her juices. Utterly and completely drenched. Sterling wanted to throw back his head and give a victory cry, but instead, he settled for a grin and a deep chuckle, which had his wife looking worried.

Well, that was something, he supposed. It was the most information he'd gotten from her all evening about how she was feeling. Perhaps things weren't as dire as he'd thought they were, considering that the more he explored her, the wetter she seemed to get. So, her body was definitely responding to him. Despite what he had thought due to how removed she was trying to be, his efforts were not in vain.

But she wasn't allowing herself to experience them fully. She was deliberately ignoring what her body was telling her in favor of remaining as neutral as possible in front of him.

Of course, she also didn't know what all of those pent-up feelings could lead to, either. Nor, he suspected, did she know what he'd just learned about her. He didn't think she even knew what she was feeling herself, besides things she didn't think she wanted to, or that probably

felt really good but were both uncomfortably embarrassing and likely to encourage him if she succumbed to
them.

Sterling felt a lot better about his marriage than he had a
few minutes ago. He had a plan of attack now. He was of a
mind that, if she experienced an orgasm—or twelve—that
she would be hard pressed to remain unaffected when he
claimed his conjugal rights again, which he intended to do as
often as was physically possible, and which he preferred that
she not simply endure as if it was the worst imaginable
torture.

He didn't think he'd ever been with a woman who chose
to deny her own nature like this. He'd had his share of
women who had no idea that they had the capacity to enjoy
lovemaking as much—or a hell of a lot more—than their
partners, which was something he had thoroughly enjoyed
showing them, while cursing the short sightedness of his sex
the entire time.

But this—he'd never encountered anything like this.

Most people would take pleasure whenever and wherever
they could, and he wondered what her motivation was in
denying herself what could be an amazing experience. He
admitted that he didn't really know her well enough to know
whether it was some kind of religious belief or just that she
found it all unacceptably shameful.

Sterling's money was a very different reason from either
of those. She bore him some kind of grudge for having been
forced to marry him, and thus had decided that she was
going to participate in it as little as possible, and that
included bedroom intimacies. Well, he wasn't going to allow
her to do that.

Considering just how much dew she was producing, he
would be willing to bet that she was capable of attaining her
pleasure more easily than most and could probably be

brought to orgasm multiple times in one session, even. He was quite keen to find out if he was right.

As an experiment, he caught a pink, plush nipple between his lips, worrying it slightly with the edges of his teeth before suckling gently to soothe the slight ache she might have experienced and, hopefully, create an ache elsewhere. And as soon as his teeth found that impudent tip, he felt her slick gush over him, and it continued to do so as long as he licked or sucked or gently nipped at her.

But still, not a sound. She didn't writhe or arch up to offer herself to him, silently asking for more. But neither did she try to move away. She simply lay there, as if he wasn't even in the room with her. And her stubbornness only made him more determined to coax a response from her.

He'd been told by several of his lovers that his voice was quite pleasant, and that talking to them while he pleasured them only added to their experience, so after thoroughly wetting his fingers in her honey, he brought them up from where they had been.

Again, he was pleasantly surprised. Her little bud was quite swollen as he dragged his fingertips slowly up and over it then back down again, while he watched her face for any sign that what he was doing was getting to her.

The only clue he got was when he heard her breath hitch as his fingers first made contact with that tiny bundle of nerves. It wasn't much, but it was more something.

"Try to relax, Vinnie," he whispered, low and slow. "I know it can be embarrassing at first, but there shouldn't be any embarrassment between a husband and a wife. This is what we're supposed to be doing—enjoying each other's bodies. And doesn't it feel good, too?"

Another slightly ragged breath greeted his ears, but it was not an answer to the question he'd put to his wife.

Experimentally, he deepened his voice quite a bit and

added a more dominant—but carefully not harsh—note to it, deliberately using her full name. "Lavinia."

That got him what he wanted from her, although he didn't think she knew that her body had betrayed her to him again. She clenched, once, beneath his fingers. It was a small but unmistakable sign that almost instantly made him spill himself on the bed between them.

Her eyes had been closed, but they opened at his tone, and he was gifted with another sign. Her eyes were unfocused, their pupils dilated.

Before he assumed anything that he shouldn't, he didn't give her time to answer him before he warned in a gentle growl, "Answer me, wife."

He felt the entirety of her private area spasm at that, and her eyes went wide, too. He wasn't sure if it was what he'd said or a reaction to what her body had done. He'd sort that out later.

Sterling continued to stroke her as she did her best to try to answer him. Her strength of will was quite considerable. No wonder her parents had just given her whatever she wanted rather than trying to tame her.

Well, that wasn't going to happen with him. He was going to make damned sure that she toed the line, or she was going to be spending the majority of her married life with a very sore bum. And he had absolutely no problem with that if it was what was necessary to get her to behave to his standards.

Her cheeks were bright red, and he could clearly see that her blush extended down to the tops of her breasts, too. "Y-yes, sir," she replied, more tentatively than he'd ever heard her.

Vinnie did not want to admit that to him, but even more so, she did not want to end up getting punished again, either, and that was more of a deterrent than letting him know that what he was doing to her was making her feel good.

It was a Hobson's choice, but she made the one she thought was probably for the best.

And her husband was enjoying her struggle. "Then stop resisting me, Lavinia," he said in much the same tone of voice.

Her eyes shot to his, and he cocked his head at her, eyebrows raised. On a whim, he gathered her wrists in his free hand and brought them over her head. That, too, got a rise out of her, although it was still quite subdued. She started and gasped, and he could feel that she almost gave into the impulse to resist what he was doing to her, but then she corralled her impulses and her body—most of it, anyway —went limp.

That was when he leaned down and kissed her, while his fingers continued to torment her.

When he raised his head, she was panting lightly, and she never stopped after that point.

She was still fighting him, in her rebellious little way, but he ignored it. He knew he was getting to her, and he was quite sure that, eventually, as he learned by observing her very closely what she liked, she would soon be unable to resist him in any way.

In a calculated move, Sterling added a third finger to the fray, after reaching down to bathe all three of them in her free-flowing trickle of slick before settling them all over her clit to rub and flick and brush them over her—sometimes demanding, sometimes coaxing, but always in a manner designed to bring her the greatest pleasure.

On impulse, he leaned down to whisper into her ear, alert to the slightest change in her demeanor or expression, "Perhaps I should spank you for holding yourself back, Lavinia, hmm?"

As soon as he said the word "spank", she spasmed again —all of her, not just the part he was worrying, and he would swear that she tried to shift out from under his fingers just a bit.

But he wouldn't grant her any kind of relief. He wanted to see her get off at his behest, and he wasn't going to stop until she did.

And how informative her reaction was! Just the word "spank" got her riled, and against her will, he would bet, which was even more tantalizing to him.

"I have to assume—since you're definitely doing that— that you enjoy my attentions. That you like the way I touch you. And the way I speak to you while I'm touching you. And you're just trying to drag it out, to get the most pleasure you can."

She made a sound of protest then, as if she was going to vehemently deny what he was accusing her of, but then she clamped her mouth shut on whatever those words were, clicking her teeth together so loudly that his own hurt in sympathy.

There was a fine sheen of sweat covering her, and she was shaking with the effort of trying to deny how what he was doing to her was making her feel.

And he had no mercy for her at all as he gently pressed two fingers into her—slowly and carefully, mindful that she might still be a bit uncomfortable from last night—setting the slightly rough edge of his thumb over her little bean instead as he filled her tightness with his big fingers.

A slight moan escaped her lips at that, and he felt as if he'd hung the moon.

The other cracks in her iron grip on herself appeared slowly, one by one. Her head began to move back and forth, as if trying to say what she couldn't, and her delicate hands grasped at nothing where they were being held in one of his.

Her bottom wiggled a bit, and she appeared to be mouthing something, whispering it like a prayer.

Sterling put his ear near her mouth.

"No, no, no, no."

Then he caught those even more unfocused eyes, intent on rebutting her chant.

But when he saw the tears slipping out of the corners of her eyes, he stopped everything and remained as still as she had been when he'd begun. "What is it, Vinnie?" he asked while searching her eyes. "Are my fingers inside you too much? Am I hurting you? You must always tell me if I hurt you. I might not stop—because that might be my intention at the moment—but I always need to know how you're feeling."

Her eyes were wide and she looked terribly alarmed at something, but he was at a loss as to what that could be.

"Tell me, love, and I'll fix it. There's good pain and bad pain, and I do not want you to experience the bad pain if I can avoid it, but I have to know. I have to learn from you what that is for you."

It took him a moment before he realized that she wasn't in pain. She was terrified.

Her eyes were wide, and her body was tense, as if she was cringing in advance of a blow.

She hadn't reacted like this last night when he took her virginity. Sterling couldn't imagine what she was so afraid of, but he knew that was just his perception, and he was very eager to know what hers was, so that he could alleviate her fear.

"Talk to me, Vinnie," he coaxed, with just the barest hint of steel. "We're so new, and you don't know me, but as long as you've behaved, you don't have to worry about being punished." That wasn't scrupulously true, but he wasn't going to discuss that now, when he was trying to calm her. "At the moment, all I'm trying to do is bring you pleasure."

Her head snapped up, and he could see that she was still crying.

Sterling took a deep breath, taking the time to loosen her wrists, but arranging the two of them such that she had no use of her right arm, anyway, because it was beneath him. He tucked himself as close to her side as he could, then he reclaimed her other hand, interlacing his fingers with hers and keeping that hand up near her shoulder, out of his way. This way, he was closer to her, she was held relatively tightly —which he knew some women found comforting—but she couldn't interfere with him even if she wanted to.

And his fingers were still right there, although they were no longer positioned as intimately as they had been before. They were lying atop her groove rather than within it.

She was still shaking but seemed to be a bit better.

As he spoke, crooning in a manner he'd used before with women who had become upset while they were with him about one thing or another, his fingers moved slowly back to where they had been. "I promise you that this is going to feel amazingly good, but you won't really understand that until you've experienced it for the first time. What I don't want you to do is what I think you've been doing all along— holding back, whether that might be due to fear or shame, I don't know. I certainly hope it isn't that you've willfully decided to withhold yourself from me, because that kind of behavior will get you paddled, every time."

Damn, she contracted again at that, and he couldn't keep himself from thrusting up against her side.

"You are my wife," he continued in the same tone. "You are my property, more so than most wives, who come to their husband with some sort of a dowry. I had to pay for you, and I intend to get as much enjoyment out of you as I possibly can. Part of that, for me, is bringing you to sexual pleasure, and I will never be happy if you're very naughty…" another spasm "...and decide to try to defer or ignore that pleasure. I will not *allow*..." a contraction accompanied by her biting her bottom lip "...you to do that."

Her head began to twitch, and he knew that, if she wasn't being held so closely by him, it might have been thrashing back and forth eventually. But he was finding that he liked holding her like this, keeping her contained, at least this time.

"Any time I touch you—whether it be to administer a punishment or to make you scream with delight—I expect you to show me what I'm making you feel, without filtering it through your mind and deciding whether or not you want me to see your reactions. You are not allowed to make that kind of judgment about yourself. That is my purview and mine alone, as your husband. Do you understand, Lavinia?"

Breathlessly, "Y-yes, sir."

"Good. Now I just want you to lie there and take in what's happening to you. But if I think that you're suppressing your reactions, I will paddle your behind, and then I'll make you come anyway, perhaps while I'm disciplining you."

He was being deliberately provocative, pushing her past her reticence, past her willfulness, until she had no choice but to obey him.

And he watched it all—every amazing second of it—unfolding on her lovely face as she slowly lost the will to deny him, and what he was doing to her, any longer.

She fought him a bit near the end. Nothing particularly overt, and he put it down to her fear, which he did his best to allay by whispering to her while he continued to brush his fingertips over the most sensitive, vulnerable spot on her person.

"Be a good girl and relax, Lavinia," he whispered firmly. "This is what your husband wants for you, so this is what is going to happen to you. Soon—very soon—you'll become used to it, because I intend to make you feel this way at least once a day, or more. And if I have to tie you down in order to do so, then I shall."

He felt her muscles gathering, felt her entire body tensing, and knew that her moment was at hand as he continued to speak, slowly and softly into her ear, fingers relentlessly torturing her eager nub.

Her hand began to claw at his back, the other trying to extricate itself from his hold as he heard her beg him softly, pitifully, "No, please, stop! I don't want this!" Then she arched wildly against his hand, her pleas turning to moans of the filthiest possible kind while she thrashed and writhed and tried to escape her fate. But there was nowhere for her to go. She was no longer the person in charge of her own body. He was. And he knew things about it that she couldn't even begin to imagine.

The ecstasy was almost harder to bear than the not knowing or the punishments he'd subjected her to, just in a different way. It was sharp and breathtaking and all encompassing, and she never wanted it to end in the same way she'd never wanted it to begin. But as those wondrous, life altering spasms began to ebb away, the fingers that had eased off touching her found her again.

And this time, she did fight him, as hard as she could, which wasn't much, especially since she was already well restrained. All he had to do was contract his arm a bit, and she could barely move.

Vinnie was forced to lie there, subjected to the ultimate in pleasure another four times, each time, more raw, more savage than the last, until finally, she heard a deep, animal-istic growl issuing from the back of her own throat.

She didn't see it, but Sterling's eyes widened at that highly unexpected sound, and he hid a grin at what a treasure had accidentally dropped into his lap in the form of his surprisingly delightful little wife.

But, as much as he wanted to, he tamped his own desires down. She was looking the worse for the wear, and he didn't want to push her—this time.

So, he blew out the bedside lamps then returned to pull her against him, spooning her as he had last night. Despite the fact that he was aching for her, Sterling was asleep in seconds, feeling very satisfied in other ways.

Vinnie, who was sexually satisfied for the first time in her life, cried as silently as she could, doing her level best not to wake him. Sleep only arrived for her after the cock had crowed, and she was too exhausted to keep her eyes open any longer.

So, it was her husband who got up before she did the morning of their second day of marriage. They had separated in sleep, and he immediately turned toward her to see if she was awake.

She wasn't. She was sleeping deeply, but he couldn't miss the signs of the distress she'd apparently felt while he had been slumbering peacefully.

He could see the puffiness about her eyes, as well as the dark circles under them, and there was a damp spot on the pillow, right beneath where her head had been while he had been cuddling her to him.

He sighed, running his hand through his hair, half tempted to wake her up to talk to her about why she'd spent last night crying. But because he wasn't at all sure that he wanted to hear her reasons, he got up instead, his gaze lingering on her until he stepped into his dressing room, to be greeted by James, and dressed for the day.

Chapter 6

VINNIE DIDN'T SEE her husband until dinner that evening, and she hadn't remembered that he had told her to come see him that morning to tell him where to go to get her non-existent clothes.

She wasn't in the habit of being late but was almost late for dinner again that evening, which was probably a function of the fact that she hadn't been expected to attend dinner for the past several years. She barely made it to the drawing room at about seven-fifty-nine. Her husband was on the other side of the door when the footman, George, opened it for her.

His face looked like a thundercloud, but he put his elbow out to her all the same, escorting her into the dining room.

As usual, Cutler went to seat her, but his lordship thanked him and said that he would do that for her ladyship from this point on. He also made the unusual request that they not be disturbed until they called for dinner to be served.

Cook wasn't going to like that in the least, but there was little to be done. The master was to be obeyed.

Vinnie expected him to pull her chair out for her, and he did pull it out, but then he pushed it to the side. She watched him with an owlish expression as he then leaned over and used one arm to swipe the entire place setting onto the floor. Her hands flew to her face as she heard several dishes clatter together and undoubtedly break. Luckily, the wine hadn't been poured yet, or there would have been a horrible stain on the undoubtedly expensive carpet.

Her husband caught her horrified look before she had a chance to school her expression into something blander, and he was glad that he elicited another honest reaction from her.

Sterling then reached for her arm, tugging it until she stood in front of the end of the table she was meant to sit at, putting his hand on the cheap fabric of the ugly dress she was wearing for the second night in a row, forcing her to bend over it.

With his hand then moving up to the back of her neck, she was trapped there.

And she already knew what was coming next.

Her skirt went up, her bloomers went down, and her behind—which hadn't really even begun to recover from her previous spankings—was subjected to swat after heinous swat. Because her butt was still hurting, she was less able to pretend that she wasn't realizing every bit of the discomfort she knew he intended her to feel.

Still, Vinnie did her best to remain still and keep her mouth shut, although sometimes she just couldn't stop herself from trying to lurch to one side or the other in an effort to avoid a descending crack, or a slight, startled "yip" of pain would escape her lips, but all in all, she was mostly able to remain stoic.

That was until he turned to peruse the side board and came up with exactly what he was hoping to find.

She couldn't really see what he had in his hand, but she certainly felt it when it crashed down onto her already badly stinging flesh.

The report of that thing—which she suspected was some kind of paddle—hitting her cheeks was almost as bad as the actual blow as it reverberated around the room.

But nothing would really compare to that.

At first, all she did was move her feet a little, counting it as a mark against herself that she did that much. But it got worse from there as the punishment progressed, and it was all Vinnie could do to keep herself from wailing out loud and fighting like a wildcat to avoid the next smack.

"Do you know why you're being punished, my lady?" he asked in a conversational tone as he continued to thwack the conveniently placed cutting board across her backside.

She answered him immediately, not playing coy at all. "I-I, oh, I forgot to come to you, ow, about the—my—clothes, oooh!"

"Yes, you did. And as a result, you're getting paddled, and then I'm going to send you back to our room, where you will remain—day and night—until you give me that information. You can have your meals on a tray in our bedroom until you can see your way to appearing for dinner with your husband in a proper dress. Am I making myself perfectly clear, Lavinia?" He punctuated each word of his last sentence with a particularly powerful, well-placed stroke.

Vinnie answered him breathlessly, "Y-yes, s-sir."

It was several long, agonizing minutes of unrelenting punishment, though, before he let her up. It was all she could do not to scamper away, but instead, she rose, squared her shoulders, and walked to the door with her head held high. She made it all the way to their shared room—wishing that she had a room of her own, as other, normal married couples had separate bedrooms—before the tears began to sluice down her cheeks.

She was crying because of the terribly painful spanking, yes, but also because, when she'd exited the room, she'd noticed that the dining room staff, who had expected to serve them dinner, were lined up along the wall of the room in which she'd just received a punishment, so as to be ready whenever his lordship called them back in. And she knew there was no way they hadn't heard the occasional verbal outburst that he had caused her to make, either with his hand or with the implement, which she'd recognized as a wooden board—with a convenient handle—on which things were cut before serving.

Not only had her husband punished her for something that wasn't true, but a goodly portion of her staff—which she was supposed to oversee—had heard her being disciplined by him.

Vinnie sank down on the edge of the bed with her head in her hands. But she thought better of that almost immediately and stood up again next to it instead, crying her eyes out.

Dennis entered the room, intending on preparing her nightgown and getting ready to undress her—not that there was a lot of that to do, but they both still liked the ritual anyway.

Instead, she ended up hugging her mistress while she sobbed fit to break her heart. When Vinnie began to pull away, rubbing her hands over her eyes and face even as she cried fresh tears to replace the ones she'd rid herself of, she said, "His lordship has decreed that I must stay in my room until I have produced my fictitious wardrobe."

Dennis tsked loudly at that. "Why don't you just tell him, ma'am? Tell him the truth!"

"Because he won't believe me; I've already told you that. He believes my parents' lies about me."

"Well, he oughtn't! He should see through their lies. You're his wife!"

Vinnie snorted indelicately. "Yes, well, I'm that despite what they said, I think. He doesn't trust me, and he never will."

The older woman moved about the room, straightening things that didn't need straightening and shaking her head at this turn of events. Her lady deserved to be happy. She'd been miserable for so long, with those poor excuses for parents she'd been saddled with. And yet, when it had come down to it, she had sacrificed herself to make certain that the three of them from the Montclaire's household came with her. She didn't forget those who had treated her well, not that anyone had thought she would. Surely, the Montclaires would have turned them out as soon as their daughter was safely ensconced in this house. She had no doubt about that at all.

Dennis remained with her mistress after dressing her for the night, and they chatted—as they always had—about everything and nothing. Miss Lavinia had taught her to read —even late in life, as she was—and they liked to discuss different books they had read or to read aloud to each other from one book they were both hearing for the first time.

The master appeared quite late—and neither of them knew whether that was normal for him—promptly dismissing the servant.

Dennis gave her lady a sympathetic look but was quite happy not to have to spend much time in his lordship's presence. She didn't know how her ladyship stood him. He was too... just too everything for her, big, broad, intimidating, smart, intense. But mostly intimidating, she had to admit. And her lady was so small in comparison. Dennis didn't like to think along those lines, but she couldn't help herself sometimes.

If she had to guess, she'd said that he was probably several sheets to the wind this evening, too, although she couldn't be sure. Tonight—their third night of marriage—he didn't bother with the lady's maid or valet roles for either of them. Instead, he practically stormed into the room and over to her, after curtly telling Dennis that she was no longer needed.

Sterling stood there for a moment, looking down at her before he reached out and grabbed the collar of that hideous dress that he never wanted to see again, using brute strength to rip it down the front, rending it useless as anything other than the rag it should have been.

Seeing the way in which the wind was blowing, Vinnie sought to preserve her under things from him, so she got herself out of them before he had a chance to wreak havoc on them, too, although she was still somehow startled when she realized that act left her nude and even more vulnerable to him than she usually was.

And she was terrified to see on his face that he had the same realization as he moved to lift her via his hands on her slim waist, walking with her—her feet dangling several inches from the floor—until she felt the wall against her back with a slight "whoosh" of air from her lungs.

As he held her there by his sheer bulk, he didn't bother to take his own clothing off entirely, just reached down to work his buttons open. Then he brought her down onto his hook of a cock, settling into her to the hilt in one bone jarring motion.

Her startled yelp only made him want to hear more like that—like anything—from her. If he had been sober, he might have noticed that he had slid into her quite easily and put together the fact that he had just spanked her, and she was wet from it. But he wasn't full minded enough to do that at the moment.

He just wanted her, and no one alive could stop him from having her—least of all her.

As he began to stroke in and out of her, always all the way out and all the way back in as far as he could manage, he watched her breasts bob up and down with his efforts, as if teasing him. Finally, he reached out and caught one with his mouth, sucking eagerly and tugging even harder on it with each thrust.

With an arm around her waist and his cock deep within her, keeping her in place, he plucked at the other nipple, watching her intently for any indication of life, but her face was devoid of emotion, that awful blank mask that he was rapidly coming to detest. So, his fingers left off at her nipple and, with a little adjustment, insinuated itself between the two of them—to just above where they were joined.

He might—again—have noticed the ample, natural lube he was able to dab his fingers into, but he was much too far gone for that. Instead, he concentrated on achieving his goal. He wanted to make her scream.

And, to Vinnie's horror, he seemed to know exactly how to go about doing so. Being impaled like this—as she was—afforded that very sensitive spot absolutely no natural cover, no hood to hide within. All of those nerves were right there, and he strummed every last one of them lazily, kissing her occasionally, renewing the slickness he needed at will as he pressed himself into her.

It took longer than he might have wanted to take at the beginning, but he would not leave off until he'd heard her full-throated announcement of her own pleasure. He was utterly single minded about it, as tuned into her as he could possibly be, such that the slightest change in her breathing as it began to quicken against her will was its own source of deep pleasure for him.

He promised himself that he'd soon have her climaxing easily, that he would train her by using her every time he wanted to and bringing her to ecstasy whether she wanted to or not, until him merely sinking his cock into her would nearly get her there. He would not allow her to ignore him, nor his efforts on her behalf. And this time was no different.

Vinnie knew she was losing the battle against him. He was relentless. But that didn't mean that she wasn't going to try to hold her own against him each and every time, even if she only lasted a second or two, which was a definitely possibility, considering how damned talented the man was at this.

He held on and held himself back, until he wore her down and she was squirming and undulating in his arms, gasping every time he filled her and, at the end, lewdly trying to rub herself up against his fingers just before she granted him his wish.

She screamed, and it wasn't a delicate, halfhearted "oh".

It was a loud, unmistakable "*Oooh!*" when her body began to clamp rhythmically around his cock, fit to practically stop him dead inside her. But he pushed past her hold, leaning his forearms against the wall on either side of her and tongue kissing her as he exploded seconds after she did.

They remained there for a good, long while. He came to his senses first, stepping back and setting her down on her feet to let go of her too soon. Her legs were as wobbly as a newborn foal's, and he ended up just picking her up and laying her on the bed while he shed his clothes in twelve different directions then joined her there.

There was something he was supposed to remember about how they had slept—how she had slept—last night, but his head was fuzzy and he couldn't quite remember what it was, so he did what he'd done before and spooned her from behind.

Lavinia did what she had done last night and remained awake, crying until the wee hours of the morning.

———

Sterling had taken Ben up on his invitation to meet at their club. It had been a standing invitation that Ben hadn't expected would be taken up for quite some time, being that his friend was a newlywed, so he had been surprised to see the older man when he'd walked into the reading room.

They went to the bar, where they could smoke and have a drink and talk.

"I'm surprised to see you. You can't possibly be bored of her already, after everything you did to get her."

"No, I just wanted to get out of the house."

"Is she driving you crazy already? I remember you saying her parents said she was a terrible brat."

Sterling frowned deeply. He hadn't really found any evidence of that, besides her stubborn willfulness. But then, she'd been confined to their room, so he hadn't spent as much time with her as he might have, although he had endeavored to make certain they did spend some time together when he wasn't at her. When she allowed herself to unwind, he had found that he liked her much more than he expected to.

She was smart and thoughtful, quick witted, and not given to dramatizing things for attention, and she had the most enticing laugh. It made him try to make her laugh often. But his wife was most definitely stubborn, and her refusal to do as he asked hung between them every time they were together.

"She's got a mind of her own, let's say."

Ben grinned. "As I recall, you've always liked that in your women."

Sterling grinned back. "That I do, old friend. That I do."

"So, are you happy?"

It took him much too long to come up with a response, such that Ben answered himself. "Apparently not. And I'm sorry. Is she not what you expected? What you wanted?"

The other man's face came over all dark. "She's... she is more than I expected."

"But that's not good?"

"It's complicated. Things are somewhat unsettled, and I needed a night out."

"A night out, or a *night out*?" Ben asked, just throwing the idea out there, to see if the other man bit.

Sterling pinned Ben with an almost unfriendly gaze. "I am married. There will be no more 'nights out'. That's what I have a wife for."

Ben put his hands up. "I was just feeling you out. You know there are a lot of men who wouldn't be as faithful to their vows as you and I are."

"I know. And you know how I feel about that type of man."

"Well, I'm sorry that your marriage isn't everything you'd hoped it would be. I really wanted you and Lavinia to be as happy as Patience and I are."

"It's still early days yet."

"True. Oh, and speaking of that, Patience wanted me to remind you of the dinner she's throwing in honor of the two of you. It's next Friday night."

Sterling looked alarmed. "I'm glad you mentioned it. I don't think I've said anything to Lavinia about it."

"You'd best tell her. You know how women are; she'll have to have just the right dress and just the right jewelery and shoes and bag and tiara."

Well, he knew how most women were, anyway. His wife, however, was another matter entirely.

When he got home that evening, he sent for her. It was the first time in several weeks that she'd been out of their room, not that she'd once complained to him about it, which had surprised him. He was of several minds about this type of punishment. He liked eating meals with her, and he was eager to establish a good rapport with her outside of the bedroom, until she had gone and ruined it by being so blasted pig-headed.

But he did like knowing she was there—that he could go upstairs and take her any time—she'd never be anywhere else. Still, he didn't want to keep her a prisoner indefinitely. He just wanted her to obey him.

Sterling supposed he could spank her every night that she didn't, but he didn't want to foster resentment in her, and seeing how long this standoff had already lasted, he was glad that he had chosen to confine her instead.

That evening, she appeared before him in one of his dressing gowns. Apparently, she didn't have—or wouldn't produce—one of her own. It made her look even smaller than she usually did as she stood there, wrapped up in its voluminous folds. Luckily for her, he wore ones that ended at his knees, which meant they were floor length on her. Any longer, and she would have been tripping on the hem.

As he spoke, he struck a match to a cheroot, taking long puffs of it when he stopped. "Lavinia, I forgot to mention this to you, but Ben, whom you met the night we were married, and his wife are giving a party for us at their house next Friday night." He stood and came to deliberately tower over her, capturing her chin and making her look into his eyes so that she could see that he meant business. "I expect that you will be wearing a very pretty dress to a party that is being thrown for us by my dear friends. Do you understand me?"

Her "yes, sir," was whispered.

"Speak up, Vinnie. I can barely hear you."

But instead of repeating what she'd just said back to him, she had her hands on her chest, near her throat, and she was bent over, gasping for breath.

His heart leapt into his throat at the sight of her in distress. "Honey, what is it?" He could barely tolerate her labored breathing, but he didn't know what to do to stop it.

Finally, Lavinia conveyed to him what the problem was by pointing to his cigar.

Sterling took it—and his humidor, which, newly stocked as it was, contained a considerable number of expensive cigars, not to mention the value of the box itself, which was an antique—and threw them out the window. Then he opened all of the windows he could in the room in order to hasten the dissolution of the smoke.

She was still standing there, hunched over, and he could hear her breathing.

"What else can I do to help you?"

"Tea," she wheezed. "Hot."

He rang for Cutler, who, it seemed to him, was taking a terribly long time to answer the summons. If he had to, he vowed to himself, he'd set sail for the kitchen himself and brew her a pot. But the older man appeared then, and he yelled, "Send someone to fetch Dr. Brandon! And bring some tea for her ladyship. Bring the whole damned pot! And tell Cook to have another one at the ready, just in case. Quickly, man, quickly! And make sure it's damned hot!"

Sterling had never felt so helpless in his life, just standing there, watching her fight for each breath.

Vinnie wanted to tell him not to bother with the doctor,

but she had neither the lung power nor the inclination at the moment.

"Is there anything else I could do for you?" he asked solicitously. But she shook her head. "I am so sorry. I didn't know that you reacted like that to cigar smoke."

She opened her mouth to reply to him, but he put his hand up. "You don't have to say anything. Just concentrate on breathing slowly and trying to remain calm."

He stayed close to her, speaking encouragingly in a low, soft tone, rubbing her back gently in a way that felt just wonderful to her.

It was more than either of her parents had ever done for her when she was sick. It was always Dennis who took care of her. Her mother and father were terrified of catching whatever it was that she had—and Lord knew they didn't care to nurse her—so they stayed even further away from her than usual when she was sick.

"Do you want to sit down, love? You look very uncomfortable all hunched over like that. I'd be glad to help you get to a chair."

He didn't wait for her to say anything but picked her up and put her down again on his lap as he sat in his favorite chair, continuing to murmur soothingly to her and massaging her back.

Cutler himself brought the tea back, making her a cup the way he knew she liked it—with cream and sugar.

But she refused it, barely scratching out, "No milk, please."

Sterling glared at the man as if he'd offered her poison and made her a cup himself.

Vinnie took it gratefully, sipping eagerly, despite how hot it was.

A few minutes later, there was a tentative knock at the

door, and Cutler went to see to it, opening it wider to reveal George standing there, looking concerned.

"I'm sorry to interrupt, my lord, but we—the staff—were worried about her ladyship."

"That's very kind of you, George." He looked at Vinnie. "How are you feeling now, my sweet?"

"Better, thank you," she answered, although her voice was still wheezy and had little volume because she still hadn't fully regained her breath. "Please don't you or the rest of the staff worry about me. I'll be fine. You know how I get sometimes."

George smiled at her with what Sterling recognized as true affection. "That I do, ma'am. Is there anything that I could do for you, though? Anything at all?"

And then she smiled at his footman in a way that he wished she would smile at him, saying weakly and with audible rales, "No, thank you, George. Please let Cook know that I'm sorry to have disturbed her." She paused, forcing herself to take as deep a breath as she could before continuing. "I'm sure she got rousted out of bed on my account. Give her my thanks for the tea, please. It worked a trick, as it usually does."

"Yes, ma'am." George bowed out the door and disappeared.

"I think you can cancel the doctor," she rasped, taking another healthy swallow.

Sterling's brows drew together in worry. "I'll be the judge of that, Lavinia. I'd rather have him come and check you out than not."

"But his fee for an emergency call will be exorbitant, and I don't want to cost you money," she stated stubbornly.

Sterling continued to rub her back, but rather than answer her, he looked up at Cutler, who was trying to look invisible, as usual. "Thank you for fetching the tea so quickly,

Cutler. I don't think there's anything else that you need to do until the doctor arrives."

"Thank you, Cutler," Vinnie said hoarsely.

"You're welcome, my lady. I am very glad to hear that you're feeling better," he intoned gravely then exited himself.

When he was gone, Sterling scolded her lightly. "You don't have to worry about the fee for the doctor."

"I refuse to cost you any money that I don't have to. The tea will do the trick, as it has before."

Sterling's jaw tightened, but he didn't say anything else, not wanting to aggravate her.

The doctor arrived a few minutes later, and, after examining her and listening to her lungs, as well as asking what had caused it as well as what remedy she had used that had gotten the attack to abate, pronounced that she had done as well as he could for her—barring a hospital stay. He left, saying that she should rest for a day or so, and that he would call again tomorrow just to make sure that she was all right.

Sterling saw him out, but he didn't miss how her eyes rolled when the doctor mentioned coming back.

When he re-entered his study, she said, "He just wants to charge you another fee."

Noting that her cup was empty, he poured her another. "I want you to finish that, and then I'll take you upstairs."

Vinnie wasn't in any hurry to go back to that room again, so she lingered over the last cup, until he took it from her hand and lifted her into his arms, carrying her up to their room and depositing her on their bed with incredible gentleness.

She couldn't believe how solicitous he was being of her.

"Why don't you lie down?" he asked, tucking her under the covers.

"That's harder on my lungs. I-I really need to sit up for a little while longer. Would you mind if I borrowed one of your pillows? It would help me sit up—and sleep when it comes to it—more comfortably."

"Of course! Take anything you need, please."

When he'd finished futzing around her and was standing there like a useless idiot, she came out with, "I'm sorry to be such an inconvenience."

Sterling sank down on the edge of the bed, facing her, and taking her hand in his. "Don't be ridiculous."

Vinnie shrugged. "It's not ridiculous. My parents were always quite angry when I got sick, and especially if they had to send for the doctor. I ended up in the hospital once with pneumonia because I didn't want to tell them that I was sick."

He was horrified to hear that, and it was another piece of information that didn't quite fit into the puzzle of what he knew about her relationship with her parents. "Well, I hope you know that I would be very unhappy with you if you ignored your sickness to the point that you ended up in the hospital. You are never—*never*—to hesitate to call the doctor when you feel sick, Lavinia, especially if it's something that pertains to your lungs."

She fidgeted a bit at his vehemence. "It doesn't always happen. You smoked in front of me when I came to your office. Must be a certain kind of tobacco."

'Well, that's no problem. I'll only smoke at the club, or I'll quit altogether."

Vinnie looked alarmed. "Don't do that on my account! I'm not asking you to do that!"

She seemed unusually upset, and he sought to calm her. "I know you're not, sweetheart. But I won't compromise your health for a silly habit that's probably not good for me, either."

"Please don't stop because of me," she whispered, unable to stop the big, fat teardrops that rolled down her cheeks.

"You'll be mad and resentful because you can't do it anymore."

"Honey," he crooned, "I can promise you that I won't, but I don't want you to worry about anything like that."

He was wonderful to her for the rest of the night, going so far as to stay awake and watch over her while she was sleeping, listening for any sign of wheezing or labored breathing from her, although there was none.

The next morning, when she awoke naturally, he was sitting in a chair by the bed with his long legs propped up on the edge of it.

When he'd seen that she was awake, he closed the book he'd been reading immediately to come sit facing her again. "How are you feeling, my lady wife?"

"I don't know yet," she confessed with as shy smile.

He fluffed her pillows for her, helping her to sit up when he really didn't need to, but it certainly felt nice to her to be looked after so carefully.

"I know I said you had to remain in our room until your clothes were in your closets, but I am rescinding that, although I want you to do so for the next day or so, just to make sure you're fully recovered."

"I am, I can assure you."

He tucked his chin down and looked out at her from under a drawn brow. "Yes, well, you need to learn to do as your husband says without argument, my sweet."

She liked his new use of endearments, even though she knew he didn't really mean them.

"Yes, sir," she replied pertly with an almost smile.

Chapter 7

IT TURNED OUT—AS she could have predicted—that she was fine. The doctor visited both that day and the next, which she considered to be tantamount to extortion, and she gave her husband a pointed look when the doctor suggested another visit, but Sterling just went along with anything he said.

His solicitous tendencies spilled out into the next week, where he was very careful of her and very nicely attentive. He still forced her to pleasure multiple times each evening and was getting frightfully good at it. But he seemed less inclined to punish her, perhaps fearing bringing on an attack, which was an assumption that was not wrong, but also not likely, although Vinnie felt no great urge to give him that little tidbit of information since it saved her from a world of hurt.

Although she was back in it when came the night of the dinner in their honor at the Meyers' house. Sterling had been very busy outside of the house all day that day. He had meant to check in with her before that, to make sure that she had done as he'd told her to and had brought—from wher-ever she'd been hiding it—her entire wardrobe.

So, when he opened their bedroom door, resplendent in his tie and tails, he was less than overjoyed to see her standing there in a dress that was frighteningly similar to the one he'd torn off her that evening he'd had her up against the wall. There was no mistaking how angry he was, and Vinnie did her best not to shake as he offered her his arm without so much as a word, but his look of great displeasure said it all.

The carriage ride there was conducted in silence, and for once, he didn't clamp her to his side as he usually did. Instead, he stared out the window of the coach, while Vinnie wished he'd just yell at her or spank her or do whatever it was that he seemed to be contemplating doing.

Sterling handed her out of their carriage when they arrived and escorted her on his arm into the house where forty or so of his and Ben's mutual friends eagerly awaited the chance both to be introduced to the woman who had finally caught him and to celebrate their marriage.

And when they entered the crowded room, heads turned, but not for the usual reason. He could hear a slight titter run through the assembled guests, but it petered out quickly.

They stood there in the doorway for a long, awkward moment before Patience, trailed by her husband, as ever, descended on them with a bright smile.

Sterling liked his friend's wife quite a lot, and he kissed both of her cheeks in greeting. "Patience Meyers, may I present my wife, Lavinia. Lavinia, this is Benjamin's wife, the lovely Patience Meyers."

Vinnie offered her hand to shake, but Patience wouldn't have that. Nothing would do but to hug her tightly—conven-tion be damned.

"I am so glad to meet you! Now I'll have a sister to

support me against these two ruffians, who are always suggesting the most improper things!" She smiled, setting her back a step. "How pretty you are! And what a wonderful choice of dress! Its understatement only enhances your beauty!"

With that, she won Vinnie over completely. Unfortunately, even though she was the hostess, her feelings did not prevail over the majority of the guests, who, when introduced, greeted her with stiff politeness, as if they were meeting a member of the Meyers' staff rather than the new wife of a dear friend. It only got worse, the longer the evening went on. Long before it was over, only the Meyers would speak to her, and Vinnie just wanted to leave, but her husband wouldn't let her, since it was his friends who were hosting them.

Dinner was excruciating, as neither person on either side of her showed any interest in conversing with her. Sterling was sitting across from her, and he knew everyone at the table very well. He was highly offended at how they were treating his wife, simply because she was not wearing a dress that was up to their standards.

And as he watched her sitting there with her back ramrod straight, obviously mortified but bravely getting through it, he realized all of a sudden, he could no longer subscribe to the idea he had once clung to—as supported by what her parents had whispered in his ear—that she would put herself through this shame and embarrassment just to manipulate him into buying her things. He couldn't imagine that even the most mercenary of females would ever put themselves through a night like this, regardless of what the reward might be. When they got home, he was going to do some digging about his wife and her parents—digging that he knew he should have done before he'd married her.

Although it was much too long in coming, he intended to

extricate them from the party as soon as he thought he could without insulting Ben and Patience. But it was they who came to him and gently, thoughtfully, suggested that he might want to take Lavinia home.

"I'm so sorry," he said, kissing Patience again and shaking hands with Ben.

"No need to be. People can be so petty."

He wasn't sure what to do to comfort her on the ride home or when they arrived home. She appeared so defeated that he was very worried about her. She didn't even bound out of the carriage and into the house in tears as he might have expected her to. He handed her down, and she walked beside him into the house, heading up the stairs slowly, as if she was thirty years older than she was.

That night, he held her to him, demanding nothing from her but her nearness, although he could feel that she was far away from him, regardless of the fact that he held her in his arms.

The next morning, he hired a private dick from a different agency than the one Ben owned and ran, just because he wanted someone who was completely removed from all knowledge of the situation. Ben would more than understand, he knew. He wanted to know everything he could about her parents and Lavinia herself.

About three weeks later, the man again appeared in his study, and the information he was given stunned him.

Sterling had been needling the guy since the first week had passed. He wanted that information, and he wanted it as soon as was humanly possible. He'd let the man know that he would be willing to pay three times his usual rate to get it quickly.

His response had been annoyingly reasonable, "D'ya want it fast, m'lord, or do you want it accurate?"

He wanted both, and he had to have it soon. He was very worried about his wife.

She had never been talkative with him or forthcoming. He had put that down to the circumstances of their marriage, for which he knew she blamed him, and not without reason, he admitted.

But Vinnie had become even more withdrawn of late. She had the freedom of the house again, and yet she rarely used it. He had commanded that she join him for dinner, at least, and she did make that appearance, but otherwise, she spent her time in their room. She rarely even ventured to the library, preferring to spend her days asleep, mostly, or curled up on the surprisingly comfy window seat that room offered. He'd spent a certain amount of time there himself when he was up here with his mother, usually in the morning while she ate breakfast and he played or read or looked out the window.

He felt as if she was slipping away from him. She had come to him skinny and had been adding some weight and filling out a bit since she'd gotten here, but now he could see —as he was intimately acquainted with her body by now— that she was losing again.

"It seems that the Montclaires have a very bad spending habit."

"You mean their daughter does," he corrected with a certainty that was about to dissolve.

The gentleman, Arnold Ross, looked through his notes. "No, m'lord. Alexander and Zadie Montclaire. Those were the two you asked me to look into?"

"Yes, along with their daughter, Lavinia."

The other man scratched his head. "Well, that's just it. I have plenty of dirt about the couple—and none of it good. But beyond the record of her birth at St. Barts', I have almost no information on the daughter at all. I heard a few tales about her coming out about the time a young lady usually would, and apparently, a few gentlemen were interested in her, but there's absolutely nothing from about the time she was twenty-one or so till now."

Sterling leaned forward at that. "Nothing?"

"No. No accounts of her being at the same parties or dinners her parents were—as I said, I have plenty to spill about them—mostly complaints from unpaid merchants and tradesmen and servants they stiffed. But nothing about Lavinia."

His head came up at that. Servants. All she'd asked of him was that she could bring three servants. He made a mental note to come back to that, but in the meantime, he went through every bit of dirt the man had dug up about Vinnie's parents. The traveling—trips to Paris and Rome and Greece—was done without their daughter. Bills for hotels and clothes and meals in all of those places that were never paid, all involving two travelers, not three. He heard about the gossip about how their daughter had practically disappeared after she failed to find a match after having been on the market until she was well past the usual marrying age—not that she had encourage any suitor's interest in her, either, he'd noted.

Before the man left, Sterling gave him a very generous tip because he'd done such a good job, but also to secure his silence on the matter, so that he wouldn't speak to anyone else about what he'd found out.

He sat back in his chair, running his hands over his face, trying to digest what he'd learned about his wife, and himself. And, as the detective had said, none of it was good, especially about himself.

Then he sent for his wife's maid, and he heard even worse than what the investigator had known, because Dennis had lived it with Lavinia.

She knocked on the door tentatively, and he got up to let her in. "Thank you for taking time out of your day to come and see me."

"Well, m'lord, if you don't mind my saying so, I was going to do so anyway."

He was brought up short at that as he was making his way to the chair behind his desk. "You were?"

"Yes, m'lord. I was going to give my notice."

He was dumbfounded. "Sit." He gestured to the chair in front of his desk. "Please," he added as an afterthought. "But my wife arranged for you to have a job here, essentially, for life. Why would you walk away from that? From her?"

"I don't want to, m'lord, but my heart aches so for her. She didn't tell me what happened that night at the Meyers', but a body can piece that kind of thing together pretty easily."

Sterling nodded.

"Why did you want to see me, m'lord, if you don't mind my asking?"

He leaned back in his chair and considered Dennis closely for a moment, then he said, "I wanted to ask if you would be willing to correct some assumptions I've had about your mistress that I now believe to be untrue."

"Well, I don't like to tell tales out of school, your lordship." She sounded faintly insulted that he would think she did.

"Of course, and I'm not asking you to reveal any confidences you share with her or anything like that. I merely wish to learn more about the environment in which she was raised and what her relationship with her parents was like. Perhaps, if I can learn more about her, I can help her feel better than she has of late. Make her happy again." He frowned, realizing that she'd never really been happy with him. "Happier, anyway."

Dennis—since she didn't intend to stay here anyway—was braver than she might have been, and she gave him the eye. She didn't like him—how he'd treated her mistress. She bathed her—she'd seen the bruises and the mottled redness of the poor young woman's behind. There wasn't much to recommend her trusting him, frankly.

But he had surprised her by sending for her, and now he seemed to be concerned about her ladyship's happiness. She didn't know many toffs who cared one whit about whether or not their wives were happy, as long as they submitted and didn't spend too much money.

Her eyes narrowed on him, but his face remained open and he didn't get all angry at her scrutiny, as many would, either. So, she decided to trust him—to a point. It would mean the world to her if her lady could find happiness, and since she was married to the man sitting in front of her, he seemed to be her best chance at it, however strangely he treated her on occasion.

She sat back in her chair and clasped her hands over her stomach. "What would you like to know, my lord?"

When she left, Sterling sank down into his chair, his mind whirling with what he had learned. He trusted what Dennis said more so than anyone else, because she really had nothing to lose. And what she'd said was devastating to him. He couldn't imagine how Vinnie had lived through it—and he now knew that there was more than the one instance she'd mentioned to him, when she'd had the attack, when she had nearly died from her parents' willful neglect of her.

They saw her only as a means to an end, intending to marry her off to the highest bidder, essentially, which he realized was himself, in the end, and he didn't excuse his own behavior in this debacle, either. Far from it.

And she'd reacted by exerting the only method of control

she had—she turned all of them down, which had infuriated her parents.

When she grew older and there were no offers, they essentially locked her in her room, acting as if she didn't exist and barely feeding her, according to Dennis. "She was to eat only whatever downstairs didn't, so she got the worst of everything."

"That's why she was so thin."

Dennis nodded. "Aye, m'lord. And she's getting skinny again. Books were her saviors; that, and teaching me how to read, gave her at least some purpose in life, and once I was reading, I began to bring her books and even sneak her out to the library when her parents were traveling."

"So the dresses she's wearing now?

"Left over from a season so long ago now that I couldn't put my finger on it. Mended and re-mended as she grew and changed." Dennis chuckled with no mirth at all. "Why, she even went down to you—and to that party—in two dresses of mine that I reworked for her, being so much tinier than I am."

That was why she'd seemed so familiar! His wife had been wearing her maid's clothes!

"But she would look pretty in a burlap sack, that one."

Sterling nodded. "I agree."

"And it damned—sorry, m'lord—darned near came to that at times. Her parents wouldn't spend a penny on her that they thought they could avoid spending. Even as a child, she had very little she could call her own. They spent it all on themselves." Her tone conveyed her utter distaste for Vinnie's parents. "The Missus always had to have the latest fashions, they ate at only the best restaurants and were invited to all of the grandest balls and parties."

He thought about the one he had brought Vinnie to, in

that serviceable rag he had forced her to wear by believing her parents over her.

"If you don't mind me saying, your lordship, despite everything she's been through, she's a wonderful person if you would take the time to get to know her. She might only have rags to wear, but she'd give them to you if you needed them. Look how, in the midst of having to get married to you —beg pardon, m'lord—she saw to me and George and Kincaid above herself. She's a very good girl." Dennis dabbed at her eyes with the corner of her shirt. "I wouldn't be leaving, but I just can't stand to see her so unhappy."

Sterling automatically offered her his handkerchief.

But she moved away from it as if it was going to bite her. "Oh no, sir, that's not for the likes of me."

"Go on, now. I wouldn't have offered it if I hadn't wanted you to use it."

The older woman hesitated for a long moment—as if she suspected a trap—but then she took it finally.

"Keep it. And if you do go, consider it a parting gift." He rose and came to stand next to her. "But I do hope you'll stay. It'll be a terrible blow to her to lose you."

"It's all I can do not to break down every time I think about it, but I can't bear to watch her waste away. I don't think there's anything I can do to prevent it anymore."

But he didn't accept that premise—not at all.

"Well then, you'll just have to join me in doing everything we can to make her happy." He took the maid's hand. "Please say you will give me some time to see if I can do that before you leave. Let me make the attempt. I'm sure, between the two of us, we can get her feeling better."

Dennis looked doubtful, but he seemed very earnest to help her lady, and she liked that. So, she nodded, wishing she didn't regret it the moment she did it.

His plan, such as it was, involved getting her out and

about as much as possible—doing things, seeing people, even if it was just Patience and Ben.

But first, he had to see to it that she had the very same kind of wardrobe that he had imagined she had hiding somewhere around the city.

Chapter 8

HE AWOKE her the next morning with a deep kiss, after which he made her come for him, smiling to himself when he realized that every time he did that, she was less and less able to resist him, although she seemed much less pleased by that than he did, he noticed.

"Meet me in the foyer in thirty minutes, my lady wife."

She was barely recovering from what he'd so expertly done to her. "Why?"

"Because I have a surprise for you."

Surprises—pleasant ones, anyway—had been few and far between in her life. "What is it?"

Sterling paused at the door, chiding her gently, "Now, if I told you that, it wouldn't be a surprise, would it, darling? Thirty minutes. Don't be late!"

When he opened the door, Dennis was there as he had arranged that she would be, and he gave her an audacious, conspiratorial wink as he walked out of and she walked into the bedroom.

She made it in twenty.

"Very prompt. I like that," Sterling said, leaning down to kiss her.

She blushed prettily. "Not in front of the servants!" she whispered, and it was the most animated he had seen her in a while.

"Yes, in front of the servants, in front of a crowd on the street, and in front of God himself!" He grinned down at her unrepentantly before offering her his arm.

He refused to tell her where they were going, but she knew by looking out the carriage window that they were on a street that was considered to contain the most expensive shops in the city. She only knew because she recognized the street name, since her mother was constantly working it into any conversation she had that she only bought things from merchants on that street in particular.

But they actually rounded a corner to a smaller avenue before they pulled up before a small place called Le Boutique du Monde. It was obviously a couturier of some sort, but not one she'd ever heard of—not that she was up on that kind of thing—and when he handed her down, tucking her hand into his elbow and taking a step toward the shop, she stopped cold.

"But this…" Vinnie swallowed hard. "… this is a dress-maker's shop."

"Why, yes, it is. And I happen to know that you are in need of new dresses. Beautiful new dresses," he said, kissing her hands and pulling her along with him. "But none that will come anywhere near rivaling the beauty of the wearer herself."

He couldn't distract her with compliments, but he could make her blush. "But what about the ones I already have?"

Sterling stopped near the foot of the stairs to the establishment. "I think we could probably retire those, don't you?"

Her face was tight with anxiety. "You know that's not what I mean."

"I do."

"So you no longer think I'm hiding my things away from you in order to get more?"

He stared down into her eyes after cupping her chin. "That's correct, Vinnie. I no longer believe that. There's a lot I no longer believe, and we'll talk about that later. I wanted to give you a nice day out, and I want you to have the most beautiful clothes of any woman in the country, so I brought you here."

His hand was on her back, gently insisting that she come with him. Vinnie didn't know what had come over her husband, and she was almost afraid to like it. But it was nice to be out, she supposed, even if she was highly suspicious of the idea that he all of a sudden wanted to spend money on her.

As if he was reading her mind, he stopped at the door and turned to her, pulling her tightly against him and holding her eyes with his own. "And before you decide to bring it up, I'm going to spend an obscene amount of money on you today, and I don't want to hear one word about it from you. If there's something you see that you like, you are to get it."

She got that stubborn look he'd seen before, and although he intended to quash it, he was almost glad she was feeling that way again, because she hadn't in such a long while.

"I mean it. If I hear you so much as inquire about the price of anything while we're in there, I will take you over my knee in the dressing room, and you can sit at Rules on a sore bottom when we have lunch."

With that, he pulled her into the store.

Apparently, he knew the proprietress, who greeted him very exuberantly, hanging off him in a way that made Vinnie want to slap her face and push her away from her husband.

The violence of that thought surprised her. Where had that come from?

"Madame Suzanne, this is my wife, Lady Glastonbury."

The woman dropped into a graceful curtsey, then she began to circle around her as if she was inspecting a slave on the block.

"She is exquisite," she proclaimed in heavily accented English. "I can dress her, no?"

"Yes," Sterling agreed, beating Vinnie to the punch. Her mouth was open to say no, but she couldn't get it out fast enough.

Before she knew it, she was being dragged away from her husband to a back room, stripped down to her skivvies—which she got new ones of, too—and dressed outward from there in everything new—shoes, stockings, slips, dresses, skirt, blouses, hats, reticules, umbrellas, and parasols. And they were all modeled for her new husband, who was the only man in the store at the time and was enjoying—a bit too much, she thought with a jaundiced look at him—all of the female attention he was receiving as he watched her display herself for his benefit. And he was unabashed about it, returning her scowl with a big smile.

The designer commented on how skinny she was—not liking it—and upon hearing that she hadn't had breakfast yet, tea and pastries appeared for her to snack on in between fittings.

Vinnie thought they'd probably bought one of everything in the store before they were done, and she would have hated to see the bill.

But Sterling had carefully arranged with Madame

Suzanne beforehand that not one word would be spoken to his wife about the cost of anything, so she really had no idea how much he was spending on her. But she knew it was a lot —a truly astronomical amount.

They were there for most of the morning. That was mostly because the proprietress had her seamstresses working on altering some of the dresses she had available for her clients to try on so that Madame could wear a beautiful new dress when she left. It was one she had picked out herself, in a pretty sea green and peach pattern that set off her complexion nicely. It came with a parasol and a jaunty straw hat that sat just perfectly in her hair.

"I can burn, no?" she asked Sterling, holding Vinnie's old dress as far away from her as she could.

"N—" Vinnie started, but her husband interrupted her.

"Yes. Please burn it. I wish I'd brought the others with us so they could be disposed of, too."

Madame Suzanne stopped in her tracks and, in a truly disgusted tone, asked, "There are *others*?"

And when they were back in their carriage, Vinnie turned to Sterling and said, "You do realize that you didn't have to spend so much on me. I would have been happy with just a couple of dresses and pairs of shoes—"

He interrupted by kissing her until her knees were weak, and she was thankful that she was sitting down.

And he sounded truly regretful when he informed her, "I'm sorry, darling, but you just earned yourself a spanking when we get home. I told you that you were not to worry about the price of anything."

Feeing braver than she had in a long while because of the way he was treating her, she piped up, "You told me not to comment on it while we were in the shop. We're not in the shop."

Far from being annoyed at her spunk, it made him laugh

instead. He had always liked that she stood up to him, although she hadn't been doing any of that lately and he'd missed it.

"Touché, my dear. Touché."

They went for a walk around the nearest park, and then he took her to see Madame Tussaud's before patting his stomach and announcing, "I'm feeling a bit puckish. How about you?"

His breath caught in his throat at how achingly lovely she looked when she was relaxed and smiling. He didn't see nearly enough of that expression from her, and he hoped he never stopped noticing how precious it was.

Vinnie nodded. "Yes, I am too."

"Well, then, let's go." He whistled up a cab and they headed for Rules.

It was crowded—as it always was—and she was surprised to see that Ben and Patience were meeting them there. Afterwards, the two couples strolled down the London streets, the men following their women, keeping an eye on them while they chatted.

Patience seemed to be a very nice woman—she certainly had been gracious about what had happened at the party—and Vinnie hoped that they could become friends.

"Are things any better between you and your wife, if you don't mind my asking?"

Sterling's eyes narrowed as he contemplated the small woman who was walking in front of him. "Today, is the first day of my plan to make things better between us."

Ben smiled. "Well then, since your plans are always successes, I'm sure you'll be like lovebirds in no time."

Since his plans were rarely successful, he gave his friend a deep glare. "Yes, well, this one is much more important to me than any of ours have been."

"I'm not surprised, sir. Not surprised at all. She is well worth fighting for."

"Isn't she just?" Sterling agreed.

That evening, they dined together, and as several dresses had been sent over to the house already, she was able to change for dinner.

The look on his face when she entered the drawing room was worth all of the hassle of getting all dolled up like this.

"You are loveliness itself," Sterling said, standing when she entered, watching her blush at his compliment. He guided her over to the couch and sat down beside her. "Before we go in to dinner, I wanted to say something to you."

He felt her stiffen next to him and wasn't surprised by that in the least.

Then he took her hand in his. "I just wanted to say something to you that I think is very important for me to say."

Vinnie wasn't at all sure that she wanted to hear it, but she didn't think that she was going to get a choice.

He turned her eyes to his. "I'm sorry."

Her eyes went wide. "F-for what?"

"For believing your parents."

She looked as if she was going to faint, so he picked her up and parked her on his lap, leaving his arms around her middle.

"I should never have taken them at their word without doing some investigating into whether or not they were likely to be telling me the truth. I allowed my more prurient desires to dictate my behavior. I wanted you, and it was easier just to believe what they said about you, rather than arguing with them and potentially losing you."

Vinnie was amazed, and she didn't know what to say.

"You never defended yourself against their accusations,

really, and I think I understand why. You knew I wouldn't believe you even if you did."

She was staring at her lap now, and her tears—of which he knew he was the cause—were like acid on his soul.

"I'm sorry about that, but I'm also sorry about this." He pulled her to him, laying her head on his broad shoulder. "I should be gentleman enough—because of all of the wrongs I've done to you in the name of slaking my desires—to let you go. Divorce, if you like, but there's a stigma attached to that that I wouldn't want you to have to bear. Instead, I should be willing to set you up on your own, with your own house and your own money."

Vinnie heard him swallow hard. "But I'm not as good a man as I should be, and I cannot see my way to letting you go, Vinnie. I can't. I have never felt about any woman as I feel about you. I don't know if that's love or lust or both or what. But from the moment your parents showed me your pictures, I knew I had to have you, and having had you only makes me want you more. I cannot let you go. If not now, then probably not ever. I want you to be happy, though, and I very much wish that I thought you could be with me, but I also very much think that you probably can't, and I understand that. I am a terrible person, and I know I don't deserve to have you, but I will not let you go."

He held her, rubbing her back and her arm and remaining silent after his confession, expecting that she would take him to task, call him all sorts of names and demand her freedom. Which he could not—would not —give her.

But she simply lay there against him.

There was a rap at the door, and Cutler came in without waiting to be asked, intoning in is deep, grave voice, "Dinner is—"

From his position with his cheek atop his wife's head, Sterling said, "Go away."

The servant left without another word.

"I-I don't know what to say."

"Yell at me. Scream at me. Beat me about the head and shoulders. I won't fight back or defend myself."

"I don't think I want to do that."

"All right. What would you like to do?"

Vinnie thought about it for a moment, then she lifted her head to look into his eyes. "I think I want to go in to dinner with my husband. I might not have arrived here of my own volition, but I like it here. As much as I probably oughtn't, I feel as if I belong here, and I've never felt that about anywhere else before. I have a place here, and a purpose, and I think that's all anyone can really expect out of life."

Sterling played with her hand and cleared his throat nervously before he spoke. "Do you—do you think you could be happy here, eventually? Maybe? Because I would do just about anything to make you happy, Vinnie. Just about anything." His voice was hoarse by the end of his little speech.

"So, if I asked you to stop spanking me—"

"But not that."

"But you said anything!" she pouted. He'd never seen her do that before, and it just made her look cuter, in his eyes.

Sterling tapped his index finger against the end of her nose. "I said just about anything. But that's one of the things I won't change."

"But, Sterling!"

It was strange to hear his name on her lips, but he liked it.

"No. And you'd miss it, too. You're always wetter after I spank you."

She put her hand over his mouth, lest he say something even more improper. "Stop!"

He leaned down and kissed her with all of the crazy, mixed up feelings that were in his heart—most of which he couldn't even put a name to, turning it into the most poignant kiss he'd ever shared with anyone.

Then he pressed his forehead to hers. "Stay with me, Lady Glastonbury. Let me try to make you happy."

"Well," she teased, making him laugh.

Then she sobered. "Do you think that you might maybe come to love me at some point?"

He kissed her again lingeringly, his lips barely off hers when he responded, "I think I'm already most of the way there."

Vinnie found his eyes and replied in a shy whisper, "I think maybe I am, too."

Months later, Lord Glastonbury threw his wife a birthday party, and it was the event of the season. Not many invitations were sent out—it was a very exclusive, very select group of only their best and closest friends. None of those who had tittered at his wife when she'd appeared at a previous party were invited, of course.

And it was an incredible success. The house was decorated in her favorite colors—sea green and a soft blue—and the ballroom was full of swirling couples, including the host and his adorable wife.

They were in the middle of a waltz when the room suddenly went quiet, and everyone's attention turned to the door, where Lady Glastonbury's mother and father were standing.

They had not been invited but had decided to crash the

party anyway, since it was for their daughter. They weren't about to allow themselves to be excluded.

Zadie moved first, her arms open as she walked toward where her daughter was standing next to her husband.

Vinnie clung to Sterling's side, and he grabbed hold of her hand and tugged her behind him. He didn't think her parents meant any kind of harm to her, but he did know that they weren't going to like what he was going to say, and he wasn't about to take any chances with her safety.

He put himself between Zadie and his wife.

"Where is your invitation, Madame?" he asked coldly.

"Well, I assumed it got lost in the mail."

"You assumed incorrectly."

Alexander—as usual—was bringing up the rear. He talked past Sterling to Vinnie. "Good evening, daughter. Happy birthday."

"Neither one of you has my leave to address my wife," Sterling stated firmly, raising his voice at a time when most would have lowered it. But he wanted the crowd to hear what he had to say, and the huge room was completely silent when he spoke. "No invitation was issued to you because you are the scum of the Earth. You are liars and you are cheats, and worse than any of that, you shamefully neglected your only child. You are not welcome here, and if we should see you at any other event, we will withdraw from that event. We would like it to be known that we will not interact with any family who befriends you or any establishment that does business with you. And if you ever darken this or any other doorway we own, you will wish that you had never been born."

Then he executed a perfect about face, turning his back on them. He took his shaking wife into his arms, feeling incredibly honored and vindicated when the rest of those assembled followed suit, down to the servants, even.

After a moment of hearing them sputtering fake apologies and platitudes from behind him, he raised his voice again, saying, "Cutler, kindly assemble the footmen. There's some trash that wants taking out."

There were cheers as they were shown the door.

The End

Carolyn Faulkner

The words "spanking" and "discipline" have always sent a shiver up Carolyn Faulkner's spine. She knows she's not alone. Writing started as a way to explore her feelings. Soon short stories flowed from her pen featuring reluctant heroes taking the leading lady in hand, but always for her own good.

Today Carolyn is the author of dozens of books. She writes from her home in Maine, where she lives with her husband and leading man.

You can read an interview with Carolyn here:
http://www.blushingbooks.com/blog/?p=175

You may check out her website while it's under construction here:
http://www.carolynfaulkner.com

Don't miss these exciting titles by Carolyn Faulkner and Blushing Books!

Series books
Military Daddies
Lieutenant Daddy
Captain Daddy
Colonel Daddy
Major Daddy

Gentle Series

Her Gentle Giant
Her Gentle Cowboy
Her Gentle Soldier
Her Gentle Gangster
My Book
The Alpha's Woman series
The Alpha's Woman
Kosh's Omega
Red's Mate
An Omega's Awakening
The Omega Within
Mate of the Omega Collection

Adored series
Adored
Tessa's Wedding

The Red Petticoat Saloon series
Grading Garnet

Thornton Brothers trilogy
AJ's Hope
Beau's Desire
Cade's Wish
Thornton Brothers, Three-Book Set

Taken as His series
Prima
Tria

Priceless Love series
Priceless
Love's Possession
Dangerous Love

The Lark and The Bull
Doctor's Orders
A Babygirl for Christmas
Her Handyman
The Hart of the Matter
At His Hand
King of Hearts
True Desires
Lord Belden's Baggage
In His Care
Correct Me If I'm Wrong
Beauty Of The Beast
Tamed To His Hand
Daddy!
Amanda and the Stable Master
Lion
The Banished King
Northern Belle
The Cherished One
Forever Wife
Grace's Demon
Beauty's Beast
Captured by the Count
Male Order Bride
Sinful
Packed: The Enforcer
Submissive Love
A Heart Full of Heaven
Daddy's Girl
To Love a Man
Etta's Surrender
Her Secret Submission
Make Me
Let Me In

'Til Death Do Us Part
Promises Kept
The Obedient Wife
Old enough to Know Better
To Trust Her Heart
Naughty Girls: Brynn and Kim
After Hours: A Medical BDSM fantasy
Droit de Seigneur
Dutch and the Cowboy
Under the Lash
The Rogue and the Rose
Submissive Bride
The Unrequited Dom
Three's Company
All Hallow's Eve
The Reluctant Bride
His
Embraced
Attentions Throbbing
Submissive Desires
Kept
A Hard Man is Good to Find
The Spoils of War
Gilded Cage
Second Chances
Patriot Bride
The Boss of Her
Forever and Always
Tribute
Caged
The Substitute Wife
Captured by Time (w/ Alta Hensley)
A New Forever (w/ Alta Hensley)
Bound by Love: A Carolyn Faulkner Trilogy

Tears of a Vampire, and Vlad's Story, Two-Book Set
Never Say Never
Under the Cover of Love
Her Guardian Don
Her Knight In Faded Denim
Forever In Love
Depths of Desire
The Power Of Love
Only Her
On the Razor's Edge of Paradise
Indiscreet
A Most Unsuitable Mate
Make Me Yours
Ready For Love
The Gentleman Dom
The Supplicant
Belonging
Hidden Desires
Her Bad Boy
All Is Right With the World
The Error Of Her Ways
<u>At His Hand</u>

Holiday Stories
A Holiday to Remember
Griff's Christmas Angel
<u>A Season to Submit</u>

Anthologies
Tamed By The Cowboy
Blushing Cheeks Vol. 1
12 Naughty Days of Christmas2017
12 Naughty Days of Christmas 2021
Dominating His Valentine

Blushing Books

Blushing Books Newsletter

Please join the Blushing Books newsletter
to receive updates & special promotional offers.
You can also join by using your mobile phone:
Just text BLUSHING to 22828.